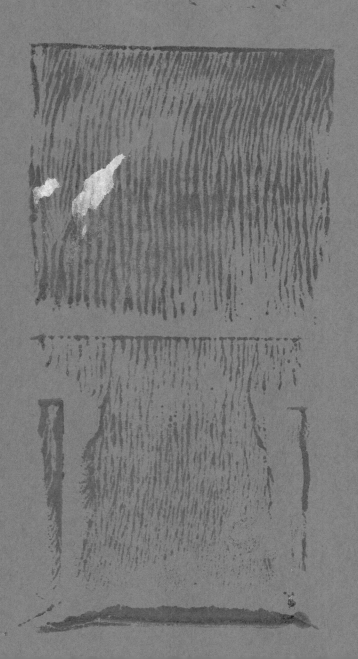

THE
TOM SAWYER
FIRES

LAURENCE YEP

WILLIAM MORROW AND COMPANY
NEW YORK

BOOK DESIGN BY CINDY SIMON

Printed in the United States of America.

10 9 8 7 6 5 4 3 2 1

Library of Congress Cataloging in Publication Data
Yep, Laurence.   The Tom Sawyer fires.
Summary: The fifteen-year-old narrator relates how, with his help,
cub reporter, Mark Twain, and firefighter, Tom Sawyer, uncover the plot
of a deranged Southern arsonist in San Francisco during the Civil War.
1. Children's   stories,   American.   [1. Mystery   and   detective   stories.
2. San Francisco (Calif.)—Fiction]   I. Title. PZ7.Y44To   1984   [Fic]
84-14688
ISBN 0-688-03861-1

To my cousin Gregory,
and his house on Union Street

FOREWORD

THERE WAS A SAN FRANCISCO FIREMAN BY the name of Tom Sawyer who insisted that he was the original inspiration for Mark Twain's imaginary character—though I have found no confirmation from Twain.

Literary claims aside, the real Tom Sawyer was a remarkable man in his own right. As mentioned in the book, he did save people from a burning shipwreck and served with distinction as the foreman of Liberty Hose Company Number Two in the rough-and-tumble days of the San Francisco Volunteer Fire Department.

1

IF I HADN'T BEEN HUNGRY, I WOULD NEVER have gone near that chemical factory; and maybe some folks would still be alive—but I guess even more would probably be dead.

It's just that Majestic Chemicals reminded me too much of a coffin—only with windows. The building was about thirty yards long and maybe ten yards wide. And it and the warehouses on either side squatted there like big, hulking monsters of wood and corrugated iron. And the overcast October sky hung so low that it seemed ready to flop down and smother me like some giant, cold, slick fish belly.

Normally, I would have walked in the opposite direction, but between the factory and a warehouse was a promising alley—crates and barrels and straw strewn all about. And, after hours of tramping around the rest of San Francisco that Saturday, it all seemed as promising as sparkling gold nuggets.

All I'd managed to find so far was an almost empty bottle of lilac water, the head of a hammer, and an old army blanket with what I hoped was an artistic arrangement of moth holes—and the burlap sack in which to put them. No junk dealer in the world would pay me five pennies for that stuff; and without five pennies I couldn't get into a saloon and eat from the buffet table.

With the Civil War stretching on like it was, folks just weren't throwing out the same quality trash. And odd jobs in the saloons and stores were getting hard to find.

So even though I didn't like the place much, my stomach was too busy kicking my backbone to let me leave. The street had been paved with planks several years ago, but heavy traffic had worn and splintered the boards so that dirt was beginning to reappear—like the hide of a mangy dog.

The chemical factory looked all locked up for the weekend like the other buildings down here.

But there was an old, beat-up red van outside. And in front of the van was a horse with a back so bowed it could have been used for an archery bow. Tied to a hitching post, it was having the devil's own time reaching a clump of weeds a few feet away from its left hoof. But the poor animal kept straining its neck and wriggling its jaw, trying to clomp down on it.

In fact, it was so bony it looked like it might drop over the next moment, so I stopped to get it something to eat.

The horse snorted and stamped its hooves nervously. "Easy"—I grabbed a clump of weeds and yanked it free—"there you go." I held it out, and the horse rolled a wary eye at me like it was expecting some kind of trick.

"Here, boy." I thrust the weeds toward it. "It looks like your luck has been about as good as mine."

Twisting back its lips, it stuck out its head, but those big, yellow teeth didn't reach for the weeds but for my arm. I dropped the bunch and jumped back. The horse gave a kind of satisfied snort and bent its head to eat.

I was so mad that I started to look for a rock to chuck at the horse, but then I saw the welts on its back. I don't suppose that horse was used to much kindness. I know I never felt very kindly toward anyone when I was living with my rotten stepfather, Johnny.

"Well," I said, tipping my hat to the horse, "life hasn't dealt you a good hand, but then, you aren't the only one."

I gave the horse a wide berth while I circled around it. Its tail twitched like it was getting ready to kick. That horse was pure spite, and I wondered what sort of mean person would own an animal like that.

The painted letters on the van's side were faded, and layers of dirt hadn't made them easier to read, but I managed to puzzle out P-H-O-T-O-G-R-A-P-H-E-R. Above it was the owner's name, but I could only make out that the last name began with BR—or was it PR?

The owner must have been one of those fancy picture takers who would put your mirror image on a chemically coated plate. There were a lot of them in the city, because people were always sending pictures back East to their folks.

A door clicked shut nearby and I whirled around. But no one had gone in or out that I could see. I told myself it was just the wind, but I couldn't shake the funny feeling that someone was watching me—and watching like his life depended on it.

I took a deep breath and told myself not to let that mean old horse spook me. I was here to make some money. Never mind what the picture taker was doing here. I headed for the alley.

The first crate was only two feet wide, but it filled the narrow alley so that there was less than a foot and a half of space left. Setting my burlap sack down on the ground, I took off my hat and began to poke through the straw to see if there were any bottles, but all I found were greasy rags.

As I wiped my hands on some straw, I couldn't help thinking that my life would be a lot easier if I lived the way some of the other wharf rats like Mac or Squinty did. Hook up with some crook, learn the trade, pay a few bribes, and all of San Francisco was ripe for the picking.

But then I asked myself what my real family would think if they heard what I had done. No, I had to think of my reputation—even if a good name didn't fill your belly. With a sigh, I began to move on to the next crate.

Suddenly it started to smell as bad as if someone had cracked open cases of rotten eggs. And the smell just seemed to get worse.

As I got my sack and straightened up, I heard a whip crack, and the van began to rattle over the broken planks in the street. I didn't blame the picture taker for leaving. I intended to do the same as soon as I could. I could always come back later when the air had cleared.

There were five windows at five-yard intervals on the side of the factory. I had just reached the center window when I saw a bright, flickering light behind the dirty panes of glass. I stared, and—just for a second—thought I saw the tip of a flame wave at the bottom of the window. But when I blinked it was gone.

I was scratching my head and trying to puzzle out the matter, when a slender streamer of smoke drifted through a crack between the boards. It curled upward in the alley like a big question mark.

I should have lit out right then, but my curiosity got the better of me. I stepped up to the window. It was kind of high so I had to stand on tiptoe, and I almost lost my balance because of the stuff in my sack.

Instinctively, I put my hand out to steady myself and then snatched it away again when I felt how hot the windowpanes were. I almost fell but managed to bring myself up against the side of the neighboring warehouse.

As I watched, streamers of smoke began to slip out from underneath the eaves of the roof and through the cracks on the upper wall—like giant worms wriggling out from under a rock after a rain.

I didn't wait to see any more. But I hadn't taken more than three steps when the window ahead of me just seemed to explode. Glass started to fly in huge chunks from the window frame. I let go of my hat and dropped my arm over my eyes, just as a gust of fiery air swept around me.

Flames flared across the alley, settling for a moment on the side of the warehouse next door and then jumping back to begin burning the boards on the side of the factory.

The window behind me shattered. A hot wind rolled out and flames dived through the shattered window frame.

Suddenly, more windows broke. Now I couldn't go forward, and I couldn't go back. The boards right next to me were already beginning to blacken. At any moment, the fire would burst through the boards and swallow me.

But instead, the fire broke through the roof with a terrible roar. Sheets of tar papers, their edges curling with fire, flew up like a flock of frightened birds around a huge, blue gray cloud of smoke that jetted skyward like it wouldn't ever stop.

My good name and even the need for a full belly didn't seem so important anymore. Why had I let myself be so greedy?

2

A MILE TO THE NORTH, I COULD HEAR the watchman ringing the alarm bell from the city hall tower. I knew people all over the city would be turning to stare at the angry column of smoke; they'd probably wonder if the fire was going to sweep through the rest of San Francisco. In the last fifteen years whole sections of the city had had to be rebuilt several times.

Of course, right at that moment, I had bigger worries, since I seemed headed straight for my own personal barbecue. I set my sack down on the ground and took out the old blanket and bottle of lilac water. There wasn't much of the blue-colored liquid, but it would have to do.

I pulled out the cork and sniffed it, but I didn't smell any alcohol. Most likely it was just water with lilacs and herbs to scent it, but it smelled awfully strong—like fields and fields of lilacs had been massacred just to make this one bottle.

Still I couldn't see that I had much choice. I would rather die trying to escape than sit around waiting for the flames to get me. I held the blanket up and poured the lilac water on one spot near the edge. But when I heard the crash, I almost dropped the whole bottle.

A board had swung away from the weakened factory wall and edged itself across the alley at a sharp angle. And the rest of the wall didn't look much stronger. The air was already as hot as a furnace; sweat was pouring down my face.

I hated to throw my top hat away. It had been more than a way to keep the rain off my head. It'd been my bank and my trademark, but it would have just taken up too much room under the blanket.

I pulled the blanket over my head, with the wet spot against my face. I took a step and leaped across the spot where I remembered the board having been. The toe of my left shoe just brushed the board, but somehow I managed to recover my balance and go on.

I ducked my head, so that I was running

crouched at the waist. I could feel the heat all around me and hear the flames crackling and roaring, as if I were running through a tunnel with cages of starved animals on either side—animals reaching for me with fiery claws.

Twice I had to stop and lift the blanket long enough to make sure I was running in a straight line. The last thing I needed was to lose my sense of direction and run right into the fire instead.

I was trying to hold my breath, but the lilac water, as it evaporated, seemed to find its way up my nose and down into my chest. I started to gasp but forced myself not to. The air was hot enough to burn my lungs.

And then suddenly I was stumbling out into the street. I tossed off the blanket. There was fire all along the edges like little, living tassels. Letting the blanket burn, I dropped to the ground and rolled over about a dozen times. When I saw sure that my coating of dirt would smother any fire, I sat back up again and took a deep breath of cool air before I inspected myself.

It really wasn't too bad. The toe of my left shoe was black with soot, and one sleeve had a brown singe as if the fire had just started to burn through the blanket, and the knuckles of my right hand were red and smarting. But once I coated my hand with axle grease, I'd be as good as new.

I was a fast healer. A good thing, too, considering what life had been like with my stepfather, Johnny.

What really hurt was that I'd lost that day's scavengings and my old hat as well. Mac or Squinty would have been laughing at me right then. Why hadn't I let them teach me how to steal?

But as I stood there, I got out one of my oldest dreams and dusted it off. I pictured the fancy carriage with all the gilt trimmings rolling onto the wharf. The sailors and stevedores would leave their ships, and the wharf rats would come scurrying out of their alleys, and the drunks would come piling out of their saloons.

And the carriage would roll up straight to where I slept, and in the back would be this gray-haired gentleman and lady with a fur rug over their knees. And a servant would climb down; he'd be tall and stiffer than a starched cat, and he'd walk up to me and sweep off his hat and bow and say, "Your Grace, the Duke of Baywater?"

And I'd arch my eyebrow and, in my best English accent, I'd say, "Yes?"

And the servant would straighten up and throw out his arms as he turned toward the carriage, and he would say, "Our search is over at last, my lord."

And the old gentleman and the old lady would give a quiet, genteel sort of whoop and throw off the fur rug and climb on down with the servant's help and come over, weeping and crying and thanking the good lord that I was still alive.

It was going to happen one day. I just had to keep on believing. The important thing was not to waste my time feeling sorry for myself. Instead I had to find some way to turn things to my advantage.

And then, as I watched the flames rise skyward, I realized that I'd been right in the middle of a red-hot news item—so to speak. It ought to make a good, exciting story for some newspaper. In fact, I'd once earned a whole dollar—in silver, too—helping out a reporter friend of mine. If I could get that kind of money for my eyewitness account, I'd come out ahead on that day's losses.

I sat down in the street and watched the fire with a new kind of interest—like now it was my own personal property.

Flames hid the front of the factory by the time I felt the rumbling in the ground. I scrambled to my feet right away and ran to the intersection.

Each fire company was a group of volunteers with its own uniforms and organization. One company was made up of fellows from New York, so they called themselves the Knickerbockers. Lafayette Company Number Two was a French hook-and-ladder outfit that had named itself after the French officer who had helped George Washington. Its firemen had helmets that had been sent to them by Napoleon III, the Emperor of France. The companies always raced each other to get the fox-tail—the sign that the company had been the first to a fire.

I took the precaution of stepping into a doorway while I watched. Sometimes the fire companies could be as dangerous as the fires. If they didn't trample you in their rush to get to a fire, they could come pretty near to drowning you once they got started.

Several boys pelted up the street first. "Make way. Make way," they hollered importantly as they ran around the corner. I could still hear them bawling their heads off as the first wagon turned onto the street.

A break in the clouds sent sunlight to shine off the elegant, silver-plated pumper; and sunlight seemed to send new energy into the two dozen men who towed her. They all wore black helmets with gold phoenixes arching over the high crowns; and on the front were large shields proclaiming Engine Company Number Three. But everyone just called them Social Three because of their partying. They were all men from Boston.

Still, those men knew how to run. They swung their pumper in toward the curb, so they could have the inside position.

Suddenly a hose rig careened into the street, running on just one of its two wheels. The big reel of hose shook when the rig crashed back onto both wheels. Tied tightly to one of the red glass lamps was a spray of foxtails—they had been first to the last fire. Their helmet shields announced to the world that they were Liberty Hose Company Number Two.

The leader hauling on one of the two ropes was a big, handsome fellow with a thick brown mustache. A brass speaking trumpet bounced on its cord against his chest. The bell of the trumpet was maybe six inches across and the mouthpiece had a funny curve—I guess to fit the lips better when the person was shouting. But he didn't need any trumpet for his voice. His lungs were as big and strong as a blacksmith's bellows. "Jump her, boys. Jump her."

And the eleven men behind him leaned forward, straining at the towropes while their feet thudded against the planks covering the street. They were all grinning as they put on a burst of speed that brought them even with the pumper.

And, though the men of Social Three were panting heavily, somehow they managed to make their feet move even faster; their pumper gave a kind of hop as it hit a bump in the street, and it seemed to leap forward several yards.

"Come on," the Liberty Two foreman shouted. "Put your backs and feet into it. You want to escort Barrie, don't you?"

I understood the companies' hurry. About a year ago, the actress Barrie Pritchard had done a play dressed only in flesh-colored tights. This whole week, the wharves had been full of talk about her return. And I guess the fire companies had been in a competition to see who would get to be in the welcoming parade with her.

Though the men of Liberty Hose Company Number Two were already running as fast as they could, they managed to make their feet pound even harder and faster. The grins were gone now as they gulped for air.

But, though the pumper was bigger and heavier than the hose rig, Social Three had twice as many men; and all their foreman had to do was shout, "Pull for Barrie." Social Three shot ahead again and began to draw away. Their pumper hit a spot where the planks had worn away, and they literally sent up a cloud of dust in the faces of Liberty Two.

As they neared the intersection, it seemed like Social Three couldn't lose. But right then the men made the mistake of laughing.

The foreman of Liberty Two pressed his lips together in a tight smile. But, instead of trying to pull alongside Social Three again, the foreman angled to his right so that the hose rig cut behind the pumper and went right onto the sidewalk. I leaped back in the doorway as the big-wheeled hose rig clattered past only inches away from where my feet had been.

And even as the heavy pumper turned the corner, the little hose rig darted into the cross street.

"Watch out," the Social Three foreman shouted.

But Liberty Two only whooped and jeered as they cut dangerously in front of the other company. There would have been a terrible collision if the Socials in the lead hadn't come to a halt. The rest of the Socials ran into the leaders, and the wagon trundled into those in the rear. I thought there'd be at least a few broken bones, but somehow the Socials managed to get out of the way of their engine. I suppose it was all that dancing that kept their legs so nimble.

But the engine could have run over the entire Social company for all Liberty Two cared. The rig gave a bounce when it hit a pothole and landed with a loud, rattling sound; but that didn't stop them for one second. It didn't seem like anything would. One of them must have jumped straight out of the barber's chair—half of his face was still covered in shaving cream, and a sheet flew behind him like a cape.

"Lay out the hose, boys; stake our claim!" the man with the mustache yelled.

Oh, but it was a glorious sight to see how the hose rig flew toward the factory. It stopped ten feet away for hardly more than a second—just long enough for the man with the mustache to tug the hose pipe off the reel, while the well-trained company turned the rig around and began pulling it back, tumbling out a long, black, buffalo-hide hose behind them as they ran toward the cistern at the end of the street.

The man with the mustache couldn't help holding the hose pipe over his head in triumph; and I could see that the pipe was another section of buffalo hide some two feet long that ended in a small metal nozzle. "Liberty Hose Company Number Two keeps the foxtail again," he crowed.

While the rest of Social Three slowed its engine by circling it around, the foreman stormed over to the man with the mustache. "You've gone too far this time, Tom. You nearly ran over that boy. Maybe that's the way they do it in New York, but not here."

The man called Tom was standing with the hose pipe under one arm, as if he didn't have a care in the world. "Besides, we're here to fight a fire, not each other." He had a funny way of talking—like his vocal cords were up near his nose. "You'd have done the same thing if you could maneuver that barge of yours."

The captain pinched his lips together like he'd just been outmaneuvered again, but he flung a hand up in resignation. "Tom, you're a fool and a braggart; but you know how to fight fires. We'll pump water for you."

I ran over to them then. "Hey, wait. It was a chemical factory that started the fire. You'd better not pour water into that place." The front wall of the building was sagging inward.

Tom looked over me. "What happened to you, boy? You look like a lump of charcoal."

The Social foreman grabbed my arm. "You wouldn't have been playing with matches, would you?"

I drew myself up as straight as I could, raised my eyebrows haughtily—just like an English gentleman I'd seen once—and, in my best accent, I said, "My dear fellow, I am not a boy." I tried to add to the effect by putting my hand up to adjust my hat and felt only empty air. I was so used to having it that I'd forgotten it was burning somewhere in the alley. So all I could do now was smooth my hair back. "I am His Grace, the Duke of Baywater."

"Good lord." The Social foreman looked like I was about to burst into flames myself. "It's that crazy boy who thinks he's a duke."

I lowered my eyelids as if I were bored and gave a loud sniff. "It's only a working title until I establish where my family is."

The Social foreman gave me a contemptuous shake. "What family? Your mother was a drunk, and your dad was a thief; and you're a lying little wharf rat."

I hated to hear that sort of lie again. I gave him a well-practiced stare that ought to have frozen his blood to ice. "Johnny was just my stepfather. My real family's going to come for me."

The Social foreman leaned in close. "You're a little liar through and through."

It was Tom who got me off the hook. He wrapped his fingers around the wrist of the Social foreman. "Don't you think there's a better time to discuss His Grace's family tree?" After the Social foreman had let go of me with a yelp, Tom's gray eyes took me in from head to toe. "How old are you, Your Grace?"

"Fifteen." I managed to gather up some pride. "And I intend to live a lot longer. So go ahead and pump water. You'll see for yourself that I'm telling the truth, when you blow up the rest of the block. But give me time to get away. I don't intend to die with you fools."

Tom stroked his chin. "His Grace might embroider his background some, but that doesn't mean he's a fool. I'll put my hose on that building to the right and try and keep the fire from spreading."

The Social foreman dropped his jaw. "I take back what I said about you knowing how to fight fires." He gave me a hard look as if he could turn his hose on me rather than on the building. "It's a cold world all right, and I guess we all need a blanket." He waged a finger at me. "But I'll tell you something, boy. The holes are beginning to show in yours." And spinning around on his heel, he began shouting at his company as if he were going to take everything out on them.

Tom dismissed him with a wave of his hand. "I'd appreciate it if we could have a good, long talk later—so would you have your appointment secretary put me into your schedule book?"

I brushed a piece of cinder from my sleeve. "I'm always happy to cooperate with the authorities, Mister. . ."

"The name's Tom Sawyer." And then, with a wink at me, he went off to bellow orders to his company.

3

"**M**AN YOUR BRAKES," THE SOCIAL
foreman yelled through his
speaking trumpet. Social Three
split into two groups that operated the long handles to the pumps. The group on one side all
bowed as they pumped water from the cistern into
the engine and when they sprang up like jack-in-
the-boxes, the men on the other side bowed. With
both sides rising and falling, I counted almost sixty
strokes to the minute and nearly got dizzy.

The hose jerked and stiffened like a snake, and Tom and the other hosemen braced their legs as the water shot out. He and his men had chosen to stand near the mouth of the alley, so they could keep the hose playing on the burning side of the warehouse. That left them dangerously near the chemical factory.

When the front of the factory collapsed with a roaring crash, they held their posts through a cloud of red sparks. And though other men cringed and ducked, Tom just held that hose, sweeping back and forth along the warehouse. And for a moment it seemed like Tom was the only thing that kept those flames from leaping out to burn the whole city. I sure wished I could be like Tom. There didn't seem to be anything he'd back away from.

It didn't take much time for the other engine companies to arrive, and before long there were a half-dozen pumpers creaking and groaning. Water hissed in huge jets from the nozzles and plumes of steam rose from the flames when the water touched them.

It was Tom who led a half-dozen men with axes right up to the burning factory, so they could chop holes into the planks of the sidewalk that had begun to burn. Tom wouldn't let them hold back any more than when he was leading the hose rig.

A gust of wind sent flames roaring right toward them. The others ran, but Tom only danced back a step. And when the wind shifted, Tom was the first one back to his post. He swung his axe high over his head and brought it down with a crashing thud into the heavy sidewalk plank.

Sparks rose from burning wood, and he must have been stung; but he went on chopping with a fury—as if the fire were his personal enemy. While Tom fought to keep the fire from spreading across the sidewalk, others began to pry up the planks in front of the factory.

When the steamer got there—once the boiler got stoked up—it sent out a huge column of white steam higher and farther than any of the hand engines. That left some men free to be sent up to the rooftops. Despite all the hosing, sparks had carried to other buildings on the block and started small fires.

Again it was Tom who was first up the ladders. He chopped away a burning chunk of the roof and then kicked the smoldering boards down into the street. And then he rushed off, shouting for the men below to swing a hose around because he had just spotted another emergency. Tom Sawyer just didn't know what it meant to be tired or afraid.

Thanks to Tom and the other men, the fire was put under control, though the factory and warehouse were total losses. Every now and then you'd catch a whiff of something real sharp—something that burned my nose and make me back away quickly.

In the meantime, a considerable crowd had gathered. Some stood around urging on their favorite company, while others actually pitched in. A couple got mashed fingers for their trouble, and one got knocked out when a mistimed pump handle landed on his head.

Scurrying around like flies on a carcass were a horde of reporters, but I didn't see my friend among them. I was starting to wonder if I should try to peddle my story to one of the others, but I wanted to give my friend the first crack, so I waited.

Then I saw the High-Toned Twelve, the last to arrive, and their monster of a pumper, covered with silver and gold and ordered special from Philadelphia. They had been trying to make horses pull their pumper through the city, but I'd heard they had trouble getting the horses into their harness and that made for delays.

The High-Toned foreman stood up on the front seat and shouted his trumpet for folks to get out of their way.

With the factory leveled and the fires dying out, Tom had the time to enjoy himself. Taking off his fire helmet, he waved it at the crowd. "Make way, folks, make way. Let the gents promenade their horses."

But even with a lane more or less cleared, the horses began to shy nervously at the sight of the flames.

"Move, dang it!" The driver gathered up the slack of the reins and cracked it across their rumps, but the three draft horses only stamped nervously. Three firemen had to cover the eyes of the lead horses before they would let themselves be led forward—to the jeers and laughter of the crowd.

Tom guffawed as the horses slowly plodded by. "You'll never train those elephants to get to a fire on time."

"Or drink or play checkers or whoop it up at a party," said a familiar voice. A head with a bush of red curls and long sideburns peeked out at us from behind the wagon. It was just the man I'd been waiting for: my friend, Mark Twain.

The wagon rolled on by and I saw Mark on the rear step along with two firemen. His arms were wrapped carefully around a vertical, silver-plated bar, while he held onto an expensive top hat with two hands.

Tom shoved his hat back on his head, and his face split into an affectionate grin when he saw Mark. "That's mighty high talk from a fellow grabbing a free ride. Don't you think it's cruel to make poor, dumb beasts pull heavy wagons up these steep hills?"

Mark was smiling just as broadly when he jumped to the ground beside us. "Y-a-a-s, well, I suppose it's kinder to let dumb humans do it."

Tom's hand shot out and he pinched the air just before the tip of Mark's nose. "When horses learn punctuation, watch out."

Mark pulled out his notebook and flipped it open. "May I quote you?"

Tom rested the bell of his speaking trumpet against his hip and sighed indulgently. "Still keen on writing that dime novel about me?"

"Your life would make a great story." Mark sketched large letters in the air with his pencil. "HERO OF THE FLAMES: THE DEATH-DEFYING DEEDS OF TOM SAWYER."

"I wish you hadn't lost your newspaper job."

"I quit on a matter of principle. They wouldn't publish a story I'd done about a Chinese man getting beaten up while a policeman watched." He sliced his notebook in the air. "And that's the pure, unadulterated truth."

Tom gave a snort. "That's funny coming from a man who used to throw bottles at the Chinese for fun."

"It wasn't at them," Mark protested, but there wasn't nearly so much starch in his collar now. "It was at their roof. It was corrugated iron, and the bottles used to make all this noise—"

Tom lifted his trumpet as the other firemen started to call for him. "Well, I've got to hop back to this little shindig again. If you want to know about the fire, you can talk to His Grace here."

Mark squinted at me and leaned forward to rub my cheek. "Is that you, Your Grace, under all that soot? And smelling like"—he sniffed the air as if he didn't believe his nose—"like lilacs?"

Too embarrassed to explain, I swiped the back of my hand across my face. "It was, the last time

I looked." I added, "It's too bad you lost your job."

Last spring, Mark and I had stumbled on a Confederate plot to rob the U.S. Mint. But when it was all over, Mark couldn't write the story because it might embarrass Lincoln and spoil his chances of getting reelected. If Mark could have published that story, he'd have been able to write his own ticket on any newspaper.

"I'm just weighing job offers right now, so I thought I'd try my hand at a dime novel. They're all the rage." Mark licked his pencil and got ready to write. "So tell me all about the fire. Did Tom save anyone?" He jabbed his pencil at me. "You, for instance. You look like you were dragged through a chimney. A couple of times, too, from the look of you."

I'd been counting selling the story to Mark, so I was a little disappointed. "I saved my own personal self from getting roasted."

Mark looked up at the sky for a moment and then shook his head. "No, that won't do. Tom's going to have to come crashing through the flames, eyes blazing brighter than the fire." He dropped his eyes back to me. "Still, it'd be helpful background to know what was running through your mind as you faced the terrible conflagration."

"I'm sorry, Mark. But I suffered some bad losses in that fire." I patted my head. "The hat was the least of them. I've got to sell my story to one of the regular reporters."

Once I'd reminded Mark about the other reporters, he glanced nervously in their direction. "Y-a-a-s, well, you're welcome to peddle your story elsewhere, of course."

Mark started to edge toward a harness-maker's store. "Times have been hard?"

"Sometimes," I had to admit. "There's lots easier ways of making a living than being a duke."

Mark took a long side step over some boards. "Tell you what then. I could use a pard who'd do some legwork for me. It'd mean free meals."

I kept pace with him. "If you don't have a job, where do you get your money?"

When several reporters looked his way, he put his hand to his hat brim to hide his face. "I still sell stories to the newspapers now and then." Mark looked relieved to have ducked into a doorway. It wouldn't have surprised me if he owed money to all of the other reporters.

I took a hard look at Mark. His shoes were scruffed and his collar was dirty and there were spots on his coat he hadn't been able to get out.

Mark pulled me into the doorway beside him. "As long as I can stay one step ahead of my creditors, I'm okay." He patted one pocket so I could hear the coins jingle. "I've got enough money for a week. I don't eat fancy, but I eat regular. You could, too."

It was the best offer I'd have in a month. True, Tom hadn't definitely said yes to the dime novel.

But Mark and I had been through some high times together and some perilous ones, too—and that counted for something. If he wanted to take a gamble, I was willing to go along. "Well, it would be nice not to have to worry about food and being a duke all at the same time. I guess we could be partners again for a while."

4

BY THE TIME I HAD FINISHED TELLING my story to Mark, the firemen had rolled up their hoses and packed their equipment. Tom slogged through the street, now a muddy mess, and collared the High-Toned foreman. "Seeing as how you boys were the last here, you can be the last to leave. Keep an eye on things, will you?"

"But Barrie's coming in today," the foreman protested.

"If you'd pulled your own wagon, you might not have been last." Tom swung his trumpet from behind his back to his free hand, grasping it so that he could use it like a club. The other firemen had begun to drift over.

Mark slung his arm around my shoulders and began to pull me back into the doorway. "We'd better get ready to duck, Your Grace. Some of those boys would just as soon fight over firemen as fires."

But the High-Toned foreman had already taken one look at all the tired, dirty faces around him and decided that Barrie Pritchard could wait. "Well," he grumbled, "We won't always be last."

"That's right, boys. Someday we're all going to be eighty and leaning on canes," Tom said. "And then you ought to be able to beat us." The High-Toned foreman turned beet red, while the other firemen laughed and went back to their work.

It was hard to move the fire wagons once the hoses were rolled up. The companies left considerably slower than they arrived, because they had to shove the wagons through the mud. But when Liberty Hose Company Number Two had slowly rolled away, Tom came over to us. He was walking bowlegged to keep his balance on the wet street. His shirt was covered in soot, his pants coated with mud.

With princely grace, he clicked his heels together and bowed his head. "That's the way a German baron did it once," he winked at me. "He was a passenger on a ship I once sailed on."

" 'Fess up, Tom," said Mark. "Tell His Grace that he's talking to a genuine hero."

Tom hooked a thumb under his belt. "There's not much to tell. The ship caught fire and I helped some people get to shore," he said, but he was smiling in a pleased way.

Mark clapped his hand on his big friend's shoulder. "Listen to the man. He kept swimming back and forth until he was ready to drop. And then he passed out life preservers and towed a whole bunch of folks at once. It's all going to be in the book." He threw back his head and began to recite: "But who is this—emerging from the smoking ship's cabin? It is our hero, plucky Tom Sawyer."

"It wasn't nothing to the pirates." Tom glanced at Mark from the corner of his eye.

"Pirates? How come I never heard of them before this?" Mark's eyebrows twitched up, but he didn't reach for his notebook.

"And terrible cannibals they were, too. Why, they'd take a chaw right out of this flabby little arm of yours just for a snack."

Mark removed his hand from Tom's shoulder and saw that it was black with soot. "When I hear a fearsome tale like that, I just wish I'd stayed in Kansas."

"When were you in Kansas?" Tom dusted off his shoulder.

"I passed through Kansas on my way to Nevada." Mark dug a tattered handkerchief out of his pocket—more holes than cloth—and began to clean the hand that gripped Tom's shoulder. "I met a fellow real eager to sell me prime land at a penny an acre."

"I know, I know," Tom said wearily, "but you didn't buy it because you were in a hurry to get to the silver mines."

"No, sir, you don't pass up a bargain like that. I bought it. And I even began building a cabin." He tucked his handkerchief back into his coat. "It was a week before I realized that my prime land was sitting on top of a dust storm a mile up in the air."

Tom had to tug his ankle away from one particularly wet spot. "You know, Mark, I'd like to do a dime novel about *you* someday." Then Tom said, "Well, Your Grace, supposing you tell me what you know about the fire."

I didn't want to ruin my exclusive, but Mark nodded his head. "It's all right. Tom here is an amateur detective, when he isn't running around creating swamplands."

So I told Tom what I knew about the fire. It wasn't much. When I was finished, Tom said, "You don't remember the name of that picture taker, do you?"

I thought for a moment and then scratched my head. "No, but I think his name began with a *PR*— or was it a *BR*?"

Tom dug one heel into the mud as he looked at the smoking ruins. "I'm just going to have to wait till things cool down before I start digging around in there. Say, what about going over to Kearny Street with me? There's a whole block of picture takers there. Maybe one of them will jog your memory. We could go over there after my company welcomes Barrie."

Mark did a little jig. "This is getting better and better. What a way to end the dime novel: Tom Sawyer on the trail of a desperate arsonist."

"Now, hold on," Tom snapped. "I'm not sure there is an arsonist yet. That's why I need His Grace's help."

But Tom was going to have to find out that I stuck by my friends. I jerked a thumb at Mark. "Aren't you going to cooperate with my pard here?"

Tom shook his head. "That's asking a bit much. What about if I let you ride on the hose rig sometime?" Tom tried to ruffle my hair, but I managed to duck.

"I'm no dumb kid," I sniffed.

Tom ran a thumb back and forth under one of his suspenders.

"Come on, Tom," Mark urged. "I've never known you to hide from the limelight."

"Your story's going to get written anyway," I argued, "so you might as well make Mark your official biographer."

Tom thought that over for a long time before he finally snapped his suspender. "And a split of the profits? After all, it is going to be my life."

I glanced at Mark and when he nodded his head, I spit into my hand and held it out. "You've got a deal. Partners?"

I have to give it to Tom. Most adults—even Mark—hesitated at fixing a deal proper, but Tom spat right into his hand and shook solemnly. "I hope this is the start of a beautiful friendship." And this time Tom was the first to spit into his hand and hold it out to Mark.

Mark gripped Tom's hand. "Amen to that, pard."

There wasn't much time to talk to Tom right then. He had to go right back to the fire station where his company was cleaning fifty-foot lengths of hose. After the hose had dried, they would have to oil it and roll it back up. Then they'd give their rig a good polishing.

Liberty Hose Company had a kind of steeple and stained-glass windows. It almost looked like a church except for the heavy planks leading from its huge double doors across the sidewalk and into the street.

I cocked a thumb at the fire station. "Do you pray as a sideline?"

"Just for rainy weather." Tom opened a side door and indicated the stairs that went up to the second floor. "You boys better go wash up while you can."

Mark and I had just finished when the first of the company came storming up the steps.

"Stay behind the rest of us," Tom warned the

ones who didn't have a spare uniform, "and maybe they'll think you're our shadows."

When the men were finished, they threw open the doors of their station and took up the tow ropes. Tom boosted me up on top of the rig and guided my hand to the bell on one side. "Now, you ring that, Your Grace, for all you're worth. Let 'em know that Liberty Company Number Two is coming."

I just had time to grab hold of the sides as the rig rattled out of the station, down the planks, and into the street. I began ringing the bell for all of thirty feet.

Tom had slowly circled the rig and come to a halt outside a florist's shop near the station. "Marty," he called to a plump pony of a man, "we need your biggest bouquet."

Marty waved a hand at his empty window. "You should have come by earlier, Tom. I'm all sold out. Some rich guy is buying up all the flowers in town."

It was the same at three more florists. Tom was all for canvasing the rest of the city for a bouquet, but Mark panted, very out of breath, "For heaven's sake, Tom. It's sentiment that counts, not scent."

"We still can't go empty-handed." Tom eyed the window box of a neat little cottage next to the florist's.

Mark saw the direction of Tom's gaze. "That would be stealing, Tom."

"It's not like we aren't willing to pay." Tom hopped easily over the little picket fence. "Jehosophat," he exclaimed, "This fence has just been whitewashed." He held up his white-coated palms.

Mark just grinned. "Well, look at this way. You won't have to worry now if you get invited to a white-glove affair."

Before Tom could answer, a little dog began yapping. Tom did a peculiar sideways shuffle toward the window box, the little dog tugging and chewing at his boot. "Easy, boy. Easy. I'll buy you the biggest bone in San Francisco if you just let go of me."

"Why don't you bribe him with a ride on the hose rig?" Mark suggested mischievously.

Tom ignored Mark and started to pluck the petunias. "I think I'd rather sit him on top of a hose and shoot him to the moon."

A little old lady in a hairnet came to the open window and began yelling.

Tom dipped a hand into his pocket and took out a five-dollar half eagle. "Don't worry, ma'am." He dropped the coin, smudged with white fingerprints, into the box and took another flower. "I'm buying them."

"Let go of my Bootsie," the little old lady ordered.

"Ma'am, it's the other way around—" Tom began when the broom thumped him on top of his helmet.

"Thief!" the little old lady shrilled.

"Ma'am, I—" Tom tried to say as her backswing caught him. *Thwack!*

Mark had pulled out his notebook and was writing hurriedly in it.

"Say something heroic," Mark urged. "Something that's going to inspire all of modern youth."

Lunging halfway out her window, the little old lady just managed to bring her broom across Tom's back. *Thrump!* "Ow," Tom yelled as he staggered into the dirt.

Mark calmly leaned over the fence. "I don't know, pard. I think you're going to have to do better than that if our book is going to be a bestseller."

The petunias suddenly appeared above the fence, as Tom thrust them into the air. The stalks had gotten bent, so that the flowers now drooped mournfully. "Take these," Tom croaked.

Mark flung up a hand in mock delight. "Oh, Tom, for me?" But he took the bouquet as Tom pulled himself to his feet.

"Let go," he shouted at the dog, "or I'll sell you to a butcher I know. He's not too fussy about what he grinds up for sausages."

Suddenly the door flew open. The little old lady appeared with a shotgun almost as big as herself. Right away, Mark caught hold of Tom's shoulder and began to haul him over the fence.

"How dare you threaten Bootsie." The little old lady leaned far back as she tried to raise the heavy barrels of the shotgun, but it went off before she had lifted it halfway. Dirt and bits of a shrub went flying into the air. It was hard to say who was more startled—Tom or Bootsie; but at least the dog had released Tom. He had white streaks from the fence across his uniform shirt.

"Hurry up," I shouted to Mark and Tom, and almost fell off as the rig gave a sudden lurch. The rest of Liberty Company Number Two, eager to get away from the little old lady's shotgun, had begun pulling the rig down the street.

Mark began to stagger after the rig. Tom was a stride behind him, as a second blast tore a hole in the wooden planks of the street. But by the next block, Tom was laughing as easily as a small boy who'd been caught writing a naughty word on a fence. "Remind me to get my bouquet in advance next time."

"Fine," Mark panted as he jogged down the street. "If I don't use it for your book, I'll use it for your tombstone."

5

WE HAD TO STOP AT THE STATION again, so Tom could clean off the whitewash and swap shirts with one of the men. By the time we reached the wharves, there were so many swells and dandies that it looked like every fancy tailor in San Francisco had been working overtime. The flock of cloth peacocks filled the wharf and stretched for blocks in every direction.

"Look at this mob," I called to Mark. "You'd think the president was coming."

Mark slapped his hand on his hat to make sure that he didn't lose it. "Your Grace, Lincoln wouldn't look half as good in flesh-colored tights as the Pritchard."

I tightened my grip on Tom's sad little bouquet. "I've heard a lot about her tights so far. Can she act?"

Mark gave a grunt as the sheer press of the crowd squeezed the company together. Every man within twenty yards reeked of barbershop cologne. "I don't know as anyone's ever asked that question before. At least, not the male half of this city."

From my seat on the rig, I could see the High-Toned Twelve in their frock coats and top hats, standing on top of their gold-plated wagon. The other companies had polished their brass pumpers so they shone almost as bright as the gold one. "I can see the Lafayette and the Monumental—"

"Well, let them know that Liberty Two is coming," Tom shouted over his shoulder. He had pulled the speaking trumpet from behind him and begun to shout. "Clear a path for the Honor Company. Clear a path or get run over."

The San Franciscans knew their five companies well. They fought each other to get out of the way. We didn't stop till we got to the gangplank leading up to the steamship.

Tom lifted his fire helmet to the rest of the

company. "I'll fetch her right out, boys." And he jammed his helmet back on his head.

I handed him the petunias. "I tried to straighten out the stalks."

Tom sighed as he looked at the pitiful flowers. "Well, considering I almost paid for them in blood, I think they'll have to do."

Mark and I were right on his heels as Tom went up the gangplank. I didn't see any other passengers. I guess they had already left the ship.

"Barrie Pritchard's cabin?" Tom asked a sailor.

"Third cabin on the starboard. And if you can't count, just follow your nose. There are so many flowers I think they're trying to turn it into a park."

We walked over, but before Tom could knock, we heard a voice boom through the door. "And I warn you, Maguire. I resent your attentions to my wife."

"And I tell you that I didn't send the champagne or all these flowers," another man said. He sounded as if his vocal cords were inside his nose—like the way Tom spoke.

"Eustace, why do you have to be so insanely jealous?" a woman pouted. "I have lots of admirers."

"You're taking a funny attitude," said the nasal voice, "considering the costume your wife wears."

"It is only temporary," the first man said contemptuously. "She does it only to support me while I pursue my Muse."

Tom glanced around at Mark and me, and the next moment the door had jerked open. Inside the cabin, there were so many flowers there was barely room to walk.

A man with a round, squashed face and large, protruding eyes stood in the doorway. "Not more flowers from a 'Shy Admirer'?"

"There's nothing shy about *these* admirers." Mark hastily clapped a hand on Tom's shoulder. "Tom, this is Maguire, who owned the theater and is producing the play." Mark held his palm out toward Tom. "And Maguire, this is Tom Sawyer, who keeps our fair city safe from burning down."

He was drowned out by a tall, angular man with a sharp chin.

"Ye gods, must this be endured?" The man clenched yellow-colored gloves that matched his vest. I didn't think his poetry paid the bills for his expensive, well-cut clothes. He looked sour, as if gold were selling for two pounds to the penny and he didn't have a cent to his name.

"Easy," Maguire advised the tall man.

"Well, I won't have anyone slobbering over my wife." The tall man shoved Maguire through the doorway past Tom.

Mark tried to head off a fight. "Boys, let's not stage a tussle with half of San Francisco watching." He leaned closer to Maguire. "Or, at least, let me start selling wharfside seats."

"This is a matter of honor, sir. A matter of family honor." The tall man jerked off his fawn-colored coat.

"It's time someone taught this popinjay a lesson." Maguire stripped off his coat and, grabbing Mark's arm, pulled it out straight. "Mark, you are hereby drafted as coatrack." And he threw his coat over Mark's arm.

The tall man deposited his coat with Mark as well, though Mark tried to wave him away.

The man drew himself up indignantly. "I happen to be Sir Eustace Pritchard."

"Mr. Barrie Pritchard," sneered Maguire.

Sir Eustace tucked his vest down. "I, sir, am the son of Baron Montjoy. I have my family's station to think of."

Though I had met a number of folks from England, Sir Eustace was the first of noble birth. I wondered if he'd recognize my family's features or know about some family looking for a lost heir. I'd been waiting a long time for this moment. Drawing myself up with as much dignity as I could, I announced, "And I happen to be His Grace, the Duke of Baywater."

Sir Eustace looked down his very long nose at me. "Bilge water would be more like it."

I had expected some form of hesitation on his part. "You mustn't judge me by my present circumstances. As soon as my family learns of my whereabouts—"

He took a step back, as if I were something slimy

that had just crawled out from a crack between the deck boards. "Where did this demented creature come from?"

Maguire had thrust up his chin and fists, pumping them in slow circles. "I can see that your fancy English family didn't teach you any manners."

"Don't pay Sir Eustace any mind," Mark whispered to me. "He's probably the black sheep of his family." Mark began to feel through the pockets of Sir Eustace's coat until he found something. He opened the flap enough to reveal a half-dozen cigars. "There's more than one way to get our revenge."

I watched Mark stow away several cigars in his own coat pocket. "Our revenge?"

Sir Eustace had been circling, with his hands raised stiffly so that he looked like the picture of a praying mantis that I'd once seen. "I am going to teach you a lesson in the manly art of pugilism."

"And I know an old windbag when I see one." Maguire flailed his arms and looked red in the face.

A woman stepped out of the cabin. A wide hat with ribbons perched over her brown sausage curls. She wore a tight-fitting vest of black velvetine that emphasized her figure, a wide skirt of embroidered organdy, and Turkish pants of the same material that tapered at the ankles. On her feet were black slippers. "Eustace!" she said sharply. "I've had enough of your petty jealousies."

Sir Eustace lowered his fists. "But, dear—"

She dimpled prettily when she saw Tom and set her left heel against her right instep, as if she were posing for a painting. "For me?"

"Yes, ma'am." He handed the petunias to Barrie Pritchard. "We're here to escort you into the city."

"Petunias. How quaint." She promptly thrust them into Sir Eustace's hands. "Do get dressed, Eustace. You look positively indecent in just your vest."

Hanging his head like a small boy who'd been scolded, Sir Eustace took his coat from Mark, but he started when he saw the unlit cigar in Mark's mouth. "Is that one of my Havanas?"

"I didn't think you'd mind"—Mark handed Maguire's coat back to him—"seeing as the two of us are fellow writers."

Sir Eustace drew his eyebrows together. "And who, pray tell, are you?"

Maguire thrust his arms into his coat. "How can you call yourself a writer and not know Mark Twain, the sage of Washoe?"

"Washoe?" Sir Eustace blinked his eyes.

"It's in Nevada." Mark took out a match.

"Nevada?" Sir Eustace shrugged on his coat.

"It's one of the United States." Lifting a foot, Mark struck the match against his heel. "You have heard of that, haven't you?"

"Of course dear Eustace has," answered Barrie. "It's where they have all those annoying amounts of money that he does so love to spend. Now, come along. We've kept San Francisco waiting long enough." She slipped her arm through Tom's, and they paraded past Sir Eustace.

Maguire winked at Mark. "I think the lady's gotten tired of being upstaged." Putting his hands behind his back, he swaggered after the pair. Sir Eustace followed in wounded dignity.

Mark sucked at his cigar, holding the match up to it until the tip glowed bright red. "So what do you think of your first taste of the English aristocracy?"

I wrinkled my nose. "There doesn't seem to be much noble about him except his title."

Mark exhaled a blue-gray cloud of smoke. "And sometimes even a title doesn't make a person noble."

6

A CHEER WENT UP WHEN THE PRIT-chard appeared on the gangplank. Maguire patted the air with his hands to calm everyone down. "Now, take it easy on Barrie, folks. Let her carriage through, so she can go to the theater and give you a proper thank-you."

But one of the Liberty Company firemen suddenly waved his hand at Maguire. "She doesn't need a carriage and horses. She's got us."

The Pritchard put one hand to the side of her mouth, as if to amplify her voice. "The view would certainly be nicer."

Hats were flung into the air, and a roar swept through the crowd. "Now, I'm not sure—" Maguire tried to say, but everyone was too busy shouting.

Tom got caught up in the mood as he led her down the gangplank. "San Francisco has spoken."

I lost sight of them for a moment as the crowd closed around her. "This is going to be a holiday for pickpockets."

Mark took the cigar from his mouth. "Y-a-a-s, well, the male population of San Francisco may not know art, but"—Mark blew smoke in Sir Eustace's direction—"it certainly does know what it likes."

"Have a care, sir," Sir Eustace glared at Mark, glad to have another target.

"It's folks like those who pay for vices like these." Mark admired the cigar for a moment, before he stuck it back in his mouth.

When the Pritchard climbed up on top of the hose rig, another excited roar went up, echoing along the wharves. Then, as grandly as any empress sitting on her throne, she sat upon the big reel of hose. Folks began hushing one another, because it was obvious she wanted to say something.

"I'm almost breathless with this welcome," she dimpled.

"Hah," Sir Eustace muttered beside us.

"I bet the Prince of Wales never did this for you," someone called.

"No," she admitted, "he never did." She clasped her hands in front of her. "And I love you all for it." She looked down at the eager firemen gathered around the rig. "And now, if my noble steeds are willing, I'd like to be taken to the opera house."

Tom had taken his place among the others. "Let's go, boys." But the crowd surged forward, eager to help Liberty Company, until there seemed to be a sea of hands and arms reaching toward the rig.

"Have you ever seen the like?" Maguire was almost hopping up and down. I think he was already counting the box-office receipts in his mind.

From the scowl on Sir Eustace's face, I'd say he never had—and didn't like it much. As the wheels creaked, the rig began to inch its way ever so slowly through the mob.

Mark caught my arm. "Come on, Your Grace. You don't want to miss out on the procession."

Boys and even men were climbing up on the street lamps that lined the route, still others raced ahead to warn everyone to make way for the Pritchard's rig. As the rig moved along, I could see her waving enthusiastically—first to one side of the street and then to the other.

"Good Lord, I've got to get to the opera house

ahead of them." Maguire charged down the gangplank, edging around the crowd to head up a side street. But Mark and I just joined the tail end of the crowd.

The rig turned left on Kearny, and I could see the opera house. It was a three-story stone building with large, high windows in the upper stories and terraces of ironwork. A row of gas globes ran along the second story just over the large portal of the door. Banners streamed down the front, and six-foot-high posters declared that the Pritchard would be starring in some play called *Mazeppa*.

All around were vans with men crouching on top behind boxes on tripods—picture takers trying to record the event. I tugged at Mark's sleeve and pointed. "Smile, Mark."

When Mark took out his cigar to talk, he had to hold it almost above his head because of the crush of the crowd. "I don't know what sort of pictures those boys are going to get. You've got to hold still an awful long time for the image to come out right."

It was funny, though. One van was right in front of the theater, but there was no picture taker on top of it—just a few small boys. And when I squinted harder at the top of the van, I thought I recognized the dusty red color of the van that had been outside the chemical factory.

I spotted a street lamp that wasn't occupied. I had to use my elbows and wriggle a lot to work my way through that crowd. When I looked behind me, I couldn't even see Mark. "Mark," I shouted, and dimly, through the roar of the crowd, I thought I heard him answer. But I figured he'd head for me once he could see me on the street lamp so up I went.

But by the time I'd shinnied up, the Pritchard was climbing down from the rig. Maguire was already there in front of his theater and pointing to the balcony on the front of the opera house. I supposed he wanted her to make a little speech.

The van still looked familiar, and I was just trying to see if there was a swaybacked horse in front of it when I smelled rotten eggs—dozens and dozens. I began to choke, and a man beneath me demanded, "Who's the practical joker?"

But I knew that smell from the factory fire. And the next moment, the air exploded in a ball of fire that raced along the wooden planks of the sidewalk.

I grabbed hold of the street lamp and held on, while men and boys were swept past by the force of the crowd.

A man fell with a panicked shout. More folks were stumbling over him and falling. The horses began to rear, pulling at their reins, and that made the vans jerk. I saw picture takers tumble off their vans. And with a terrible scream, the Pritchard fell from the rig into the mob.

Tom suddenly appeared on top of his company's rig, so I knew he was all right. Mark was clinging with both arms to my street lamp. "Tom's okay," I shouted down to him.

Mark squeezed the street lamp as the frightened crowd surged around us. "But where's the Pritchard?"

I could see some soldiers and firemen and policemen trying to fight their way to her through the mob; but all her rescuers did was pack folks in more tightly. All Sir Eustace could do was jump up and down and shout. I thought for sure the Prichard was going to be crushed.

And then, suddenly Tom jumped down from the rig. The next moment, he had reappeared with the Pritchard in his arms. "Tom's got her," I cried down to Mark.

Holding the Pritchard tightly against his chest, Tom climbed back up on the rig and started to bellow in a voice that would carry through any crowd. "Jump her, Liberty Company. Jump her."

I just hoped someone had taken a picture of it, because you couldn't have asked for a better pose. I started to wave one hand. "That's my partner, Tom Sawyer, up there. That's him saving the Pritchard."

People stopped shoving and turned to look at Tom. And standing up there so tall and handsome and confident, Tom just made you feel that things were going to be all right.

Folks started to cheer, even while he was

shouting directions to his company to pull the rig to safer ground. And I found myself joining in.

A bell was beginning to ring in the watchtower. Someone had stayed on duty and hadn't gone off to gawk at the Pritchard. I could see the other uniformed firemen racing off—purposefully now, to get their wagons and rigs.

Tom had set the Pritchard back on her feet and then jumped down. "You," he shouted, "and you." He grabbed two men by their collars. "Help me form a bucket brigade to the theater." Tom began to form a long line that stretched across the sidewalk into an alley by the opera house—and I guess through a side door into the theater itself.

In the distance, I could see the pumpers trying to work themselves into a line that would reach from the cistern to the theater, but it was hard moving anything through that crowded street. Only Tom seemed to be able to get folks to listen.

When Tom threw the contents out of the first bucket onto the fire, I saw the sand flying out. Tom was using his head again. Other men were hurrying to fill pails with dirt from the alley by the opera house. "He's using sand to put out the fire," I shouted down to Mark.

"It'll make a great chapter—if we live that long." Mark's hat was dented and his cigar was broken and he was covered with dirt. "The only real damage is to my cigar." He flung it away and then felt his pocket; and his face took on a forlorn look.

"Or rather, my cigars." He dipped a hand in his pocket and held up a handful of crushed and broken cigars. There was only one undamaged one left.

"Crime doesn't pay."

Still hugging the street lamp, Mark took out his notebook. "We'd better get the details down while they're fresh."

But I was silent for a moment, watching as the red van slowly moved away. In a space cleared by the crowd, I could see that the swaybacked horse was pulling it.

7

I T TOOK ABOUT AN HOUR FOR TOM TO GET FREE of the reporters and examine the black circle that covered part of the sidewalk and the street in front of the theater. "There's something mighty suspicious about this fire."

Mark studied Tom's face eagerly. "So you think there really is an arsonist loose in San Francisco?"

Tom nodded grimly. "And one who knows his business."

I dug my heel through the sand, and the blackened planks collapsed under my shoe. "I smelled rotten eggs again, just like that last fire."

Tom's chin sank down against his chest. "Well, the rotten-egg smell would be hydrogen sulfide—probably in solution. That stuff evaporates real quick once it's exposed to the air." He pushed out his lips and gave a puff. "Just like that. You put some incendiary agent—like phosphor—into the solution. When the solution evaporates, the agent makes contact with the air and bursts into flame."

"Where would someone get that stuff?" Mark asked.

"Any decent-sized chemical factory ought to have the things you'd need."

"But why start a fire during the parade?" I wondered.

Mark jotted something down quickly in his notebook. "Maybe it was a warning—kind of like a calling card," said Mark.

Tom shook his head. "We won't know till we find that arsonist."

Mark held up his pencil. "Our steely-eyed hero knew he must take decisive action, and quickly, so—"

Tom turned his back on Mark. "Well, this particular steely-eyed hero is going to Maguire's office in the theater. He ought to have a city directory* there. That could save us some time

*Before the invention of telephones, San Francisco had an address book called the city directory.

looking for whoever is the picture taker."

Entering through a side door on the alley, we wandered into a gaslit hallway filled with rolls of canvas and the wooden cutouts of rocks and such. "What are these for, anyway?"

"Backdrops and props—to make you think you're there," Mark explained. "Haven't you ever seen a play?"

"I've read about them," I said cautiously, afraid that Mark might poke fun at me. But by now I should have known him better. Mark had a soft spot in his heart for his friends.

"Well, we'll go see one . . . but maybe one less . . . um . . . educational than the Pritchard's play."

Mark turned into a corridor that was dark except for the light that came through one door's frosted plate-glass window. Behind it we could see a silhouette; but it wasn't Maguire's bulky figure. Rather, it was a little stick of a woman with her hair done up in a bun.

Mark knocked on the door really loud. "Hello?"

It seemed to me that the woman gave a jump. At any rate, she hesitated a little longer than she should have before she said, "Come in." She had a voice that rang like fine china, and there was a trace of Irish brogue.

"We're okay. It's Letty. She handles the wardrobe department." Mark swung the door open to reveal a huge mahogany desk, and behind the desk was a small woman with thick glasses. I couldn't see how she could be a seamstress for long, with eyes as bad as that.

She was dressed in a fancy pleated blouse and corsage bodice with braid and lace, and a skirt with geometric designs embroidered on the bottom along with ruffles. It seemed more like a dress for a governess than a seamstress.

Mark hastily snatched the hat from his head. "Afternoon, Letty. I hope we're not interrupting anything."

"Well, if it isn't Mister Mark Twain." Letty slammed the big ledger book shut.

When I'd first seen her, I'd thought she had the no-nonsense look of a schoolteacher. But her mouth softened now into a little smile—as if she couldn't stay mad at Mark for very long.

Encouraged, Mark strolled into the office. "You're always working, Letty. Maguire ought to pay you for two people."

Tom and I trailed Mark cautiously. He didn't seem to have any trouble navigating through the mess in the office, but neither Tom nor I were as familiar with it as he seemed to be. Framed theatrical posters were hanging crookedly on the walls, and, though all the furniture was the heavy, expensive kind, most of it was covered with stacks of old programs, scripts, papers, and even costumes.

She reached behind her and, with the elegance of a duchess, lifted a green shawl from the back of the chair as if it were really a cape lined with gold. "It'd please me if the Great Maguire paid me for one person."

I glanced down at the desk. Most of the papers there seemed to be second and third notices for bills. Apparently, Maguire and Mark handled their debts the same way.

"Well, the money should come rolling in once the Pritchard starts cavorting." Mark reached a hand over to help Letty free her shawl from where it had snagged on a drawer knob.

She acknowledged the gesture with a gracious nod of her head. "In the meantime, I'm going to have lunch, now that I've brought the costume inventory up to date. Will you join me? There's enough for two . . . or"—she studied Tom and me—"four."

Mark perched on the desk, one foot swinging free in the air. "This is my partner, Tom Sawyer."

"You're quite the hero," Letty congratulated him.

Mark swung his hand toward me. "And this is His Grace, the Duke of Baywater."

"Oh?" Letty leaned her head toward her shoulder, as she examined me even more closely. There was something about her gray eyes that suggested she missed very little about a person. And I got ready for her to laugh at me like all the others had. But instead, she rose up enough from the chair to drop a little curtsy. "Well, I've never met a real duke before. If I'd known you were coming, I'd have packed a better lunch. It's just ham and cheese sandwiches." She sat back down again.

"You won't throw me into your dungeons, will you? I might mildew."

Putting one arm over my stomach and the other behind my back, I bowed low and used my best accent. "It's the company, not the food that makes for a banquet."

Letty fluttered a hand in front of her face as if she needed cool air. "Well, now, aren't you the charmer? But it's too early to get me drunk on flattery."

I eyed her suspiciously, to see if she was teasing, but she seemed perfectly sincere.

Letty sighed. "I've always wanted to travel to Europe and see all those wonderful cities and castles instead of just reading about them."

"It's as good a dream as any," I allowed.

She dipped her hand and looked at me meaningfully. "And everyone should have at least one dream. Most folks don't know they have the wings to fly."

I didn't usually warm up to folks quick, but I felt I could trust Letty. "I know," I agreed. "Folks just insist on walking instead of trying their wings."

"You run the risk of taking some bad spills, trying those wings," Mark cautioned.

"When I've come into my own," I promised Letty, "you'll be an honored guest on my estate."

Mark rested his hands on one knee. "Then maybe I'd better give a full introduction. Your

Grace, this is Letitia Cleary—the fastest needle west of the Mississippi."

Letty tapped the tip of Mark's nose. "No faster than your tongue, Mark. I expect you to bring me up to date on all your adventures."

Mark held up his shoe, so we could see the hole in the sole, and gave a relaxed, easy laugh for the first time that day—he didn't have to put on a show for Letty. "It's mostly walking all over the city peeking through keyholes."

Letty put the cover on the inkwell. "Don't disillusion me, Mark." She lifted her head, exposing a white throat. "When I'm sitting in my little cubbyhole sewing on sequins, I like to think of you doing all kinds of exciting things." She leaned forward to peer at a tear on Mark's coat. "Oh, dear, you'd better let me do some emergency repair work on your coat." She put her hand up to the side of her high collar and took out a needle and thread that had been stuck into it.

Mark tapped the pencil in his coat pocket. "And I thought *I* traveled close to my work."

"You never know when some crisis might come up." Letty motioned for Mark to take his coat off. "Now, come on. It won't take more than a few seconds."

Mark shrugged off his coat. "I'm mighty obliged to you, Letty."

Letty set the coat on her lap. "Oh, I'm always taking in strays."

Mark examined a pile of papers. "Speaking of strays, have you seen the city directory?"

Letty peered at the desk. "I saw it around here . . . yes." She eased the directory out from under a stack of papers to her right and handed it to Mark. "What are you looking up?"

"Oh, just an address." He passed the book to me. "Here. See if you can find anything familiar in that, while Letty and I catch up on things. And after that, I'll let Letty treat you to lunch."

Letty slid the needle into the frayed part of Mark's coat. "Will you let me show His Grace my little kingdom in the wardrobe room?"

"Kingdom?" I asked, as I opened the directory.

"I've costumes of kings and queens from all countries and times. It's silly, I know, but sometimes I can almost imagine people inside them. Richard the Lionhearted. Cleopatra."

The more I knew Letty, the more I liked her. "Any friend of yours is a friend of mine."

"I hope you'll keep the socializing till after lunch." Mark held out his thumb to us. "Don't let her fool you, boys. Letty serves slices of ham as thick as this. There'll be enough for all."

Letty picked up her sewing. "It's the advantage of having a cousin with a smokehouse."

Mark patted his stomach as if he were really looking forward to lunch. "You've got a mighty fine taste in relatives."

While I was flipping through the pages, I glanced at Letty from the corner of my eye. Her needle was flying as she talked. "I've hardly seen him. Or anyone." She arched her eyebrows. "We've been working overtime to get all the costumes ready for this show."

Mark held one hand on his waist and the other on his neck. "I wouldn't think the Pritchard's costume would be all that hard to make."

Letty rolled her eyes and sighed melodramatically. "She doesn't wear much, but it all has to be strategic. She's supposed to be a Tartar prince by the name of Mazeppa."

Mark scrutinized one of the posters for the play. It showed a long-haired woman tied to the back of a horse. "You'd think they'd give her more than flesh-colored tights and a shirt no bigger than a baby's diaper."

I turned the directory pages to the B's. "But see here, wouldn't the Tartars know she wasn't a boy once they had her shirt off?"

"Humph." Letty began to sew a little slower. "Maguire knows a good gimmick when he's got one. They're all supposed to be as nearsighted as me, I guess."

"Well, don't keep us in suspense, Letty." Mark twisted his head to examine the progress of the repairs. "What else happens?"

Letty shoved Mark's head back, so he wouldn't block her light. "Shame on you. A literary man like yourself and you don't know the story of Prince Mazeppa?"

"I have to admit it's a hole in my education."

Mark began to kick his leg up and down. "But I don't think I could match you, anyway, Letty. You read more than anyone I've ever met."

"It's what comes of a misspent girlhood. Oh, here's another tear. I'm going to report you for cruelty to your coat, Mark." And while Letty went on sewing, she told us the story.

"Mazeppa was supposed to be a prince of the Tartars, who were a kind of hard-breathing cavalry outfit who went ripping and roaring around not letting folks sleep. (They actually sounded a little like firemen off-duty.) So naturally, when the prince falls in love with a Polish girl, her family objects. Well, sir, the Poles tie poor Mazeppa to the back of a horse and send the prince galloping off onto the stage."

I had the directory in front of me. When I didn't have luck with the B's, I tried the P's. "Seems to me they could get a woman who knows how to ride a horse properly, so they wouldn't have to tie her down."

"The audience isn't interested in horsemanship at that point," Mark chuckled.

In her excitement, Letty's hand with the needle shot into the air. "If you're looking for better quality, I've been introduced to a spine-tingling writer. But maybe you know him already? A Southerner by the name of Poe?"

Mark scratched his head. "Can't say that I have. How did you hear about him?"

"Oh, my brother's employer, Mr. Prescott, gave

Poe's book to me." Letty massaged the needle between her fingers. "He's quite well read—even courtly. I think he's going to be such a good influence on my brother Bobby."

Mark pursed his lips and nodded his head as if he were glad to hear that bit of news. "Bobby's all right, then?"

"Yes, he's over—she hesitated with a glance at us—"over his problem. In fact," she added proudly, "Mr. Prescott says he has a natural eye for photography. I think he's finally put his past behind him."

My finger paused in the middle of one column of *P*'s. "Prescott?"

Letty leaned forward conspiratorially. "I suppose you can keep a secret. Bobby asked me to loan him some costumes. He and Mr. Prescott have an idea for a special series of pictures. I was just doctoring the ledger books so Maguire wouldn't know."

If Bobby was mixed up with the picture taker we were looking for, I wasn't sure how "over his problem" he was. But Letty misunderstood, when she saw the three of us exchanging doubtful looks. "It isn't stealing. Just borrowing. Besides, many's the time—like now—that I've had to work for my salary."

Mark held up his hand hastily. "Yes, of course, Letty. We're not blaming you." He shot warning glances at both Tom and me. I suppose he didn't want to alarm Letty before we were sure. "Just when is Mr. Prescott supposed to come by for the costumes?''

Letty tied up the last stitch. "An hour ago, but perhaps all the hullabaloo kept him away. He's usually very prompt."

Tom rubbed a finger down his throat speculatively. "I was thinking of sending some photographs back home to New York. Just where is this Mr. Prescott?"

"Six thirty-one Kearny." Letty stuck the needle back into her collar and held the coat up for Mark. "There. I won't say it's as good as new, but it's as good as I can make it."

Tom snatched up the coat and thrust it into Mark's arms. "Let's go."

"My, you are in a hurry." Letty rose. "Well, let me give you those sandwiches. You can eat them on your way." She slid around the desk and patted Mark's arm. "And I can loan you my copy of Poe. Your education's been neglected long enough."

"I don't know how we're going to repay you," Mark said.

"Just say hello to Bobby." Letty smiled.

"We'll do that," Tom promised quietly. "And maybe more."

8

L
ETTY'S SANDWICHES WERE EVERY BIT AS good as Mark had said, and we finished them in just a couple of blocks. By the time we reached Market Street, there was a wind kicking up the dust from where the planks had worn away. Talking, let alone eating, brought in mouthfuls of dirt. Mark clapped one hand over his hat. "And they call Chicago the Windy City." He shoved Letty's copy of Poe farther down in his coat pocket.

We walked toward the bay until we reached Second Street. There we turned south down a busy little street. Most of the buildings were two and three stories. The lower story had grocery or milliner or tailor or stationery shops, while the upper floors seemed to be rooms for rent. And beyond I could see the roofs and towers of the rich people's mansions.

Most of the people on the street walked with a brisk pace, as if they didn't have much time for their errands.

As I counted off the numbers, I felt my insides twisting. We all stopped a few yards away from 631 Kearny. The sign above the store window said PHOTOGRAPHER, but there wasn't any name of the owner. There were about a dozen framed pictures on stands in front of a curtain—men and women in their Sunday best trying to look serious and hopeful and ending up looking like fugitives from a funeral.

"Do you think this is it?" I asked.

"Let's find out," Tom said. There was a CLOSED sign on the door, but Tom tried it, anyway. It was locked.

"Let's come back later." Mark sounded relieved.

"Wait. I don't see the van. Let's see what other evidence we can find inside."

"What if someone sees us?" Mark hissed. I slipped around the side past some old trash, and

I could hear Mark and Tom crashing after me.

"We'll just tell them we came by to pick up some pictures," Tom replied.

But there wasn't much to see behind the house— just stairs and back porches with clotheslines, from which a patched union suit flapped like a tired flag.

Marching straight to the back door of the store, I tried the doorknob and rattled it. "It's locked."

"Leave this to me, pard." Tom hipped me out of his way while he dug a penknife out of his pocket. "Mark, you can quote me: Tom Sawyer will stop at nothing to bring an arch-criminal to justice."

Mark peered down the alley as if a horde of policemen were going to come charging down it in another second. "Tom Sawyer," he hissed urgently, "don't tell me how to write your life. This is breaking and entering."

"We'll lock up after we leave." Tom stuck his tongue out of a corner of his mouth while he jiggled his knife. "There we go." With a little shove of his hand, he pushed the door open. Light came dimly through the window curtains to show half-eaten food on the table and old clothes on the floor. A bed sat in one corner with a blanket hanging half onto the floor. The only decoration was newspaper clippings nailed to the wall. More newspapers were piled on the floor. There was also an odd, narrow room of unpainted wood—more like a shed than a room.

"What's in here?" Tom walked over to the door and twisted the knob. Inside were bottles of chemicals and trays on a table.

Mark peered over his shoulder. "This is probably where he develops his pictures."

"I'll check the front," I said, and pushed through the curtain that covered the doorway, but there was only a kind of backdrop and a chair and a few other props like a pedestal. I poked around among the props, but there wasn't anything special about them or the photographs on the wall—except for the fact that the frames were dusty and the pictures were beginning to fade.

I had started for the curtain again, when I felt something cling to the sole of my shoe. I bent and touched the first of a series of small black spots. I raised my fingers and rubbed the black stuff between my fingertips. "This is tar."

Tom came into the front room and squatted down beside me. "Like at shipyards."

Mark hovered in the doorway. "Have there been any fires there lately?"

Tom rose and looked around at the props, but he didn't see anything more than I had. "No. And not on the waterfront, either."

"Well, what about Tar Flat?" Mark asked. Tar Flat was what folks called the area around the gasworks, because one of the by-products of making gas was a sticky kind of tar.

"That could be," Tom allowed. "But how did you think of that?"

"Look at what I found." Mark spread out a pile of photographs on the floor. The first one was a dark, murky picture of some factory building—almost as if it were night. The next one was of the same building, but less dark. And the one after that was even less dark. And then there were several pictures that got progressively lighter, until the building almost seemed to fade from view. "I think these are all pictures of the gasworks, but they're either under- or overexposed."

Tom scratched his head. "The pictures look fuzzy, too."

"Amateurish." Mark arranged the photos from the darkest to the lightest. When he finished, he swept his finger along one column of pictures. "Look at this fellow in the derby. He's heading into the gasworks with a length of pipe."

I pointed to a lighter photograph. "And here he's leaving, but he doesn't have the pipe now."

Tom got excited. He sat back on his heels and indicated all the pictures with a sweep of his hand. "These were taken at different times of the same scene."

I tapped the nearest picture. "I'd say they were all taken on the same day. But why is the lighting so different?"

Mark got up and dusted off his knees. "Maybe he was experimenting with different exposure times, just to see what would happen. But why of the gasworks?"

"Maybe for sabotage." Mark picked up one of

the better pictures and studied it. "Remember that bottle of Greek Fire the Confederate had when we caught up with him?"

When the Confederate raiders had been trying to make their getaway, one of them had threatened to set fire to our ship. "You mean, the major bought chemicals from Prescott?"

Mark nodded toward the chemicals in the developing room. "What better cover? Who'd think twice if a photographer carted chemicals around?" He made a quick note in his notebook. "This story is getting better and better. Tom Sawyer, hot on the trail of an arch-criminal. We'll sell a million copies."

Tom drew his eyebrows together. "Just what are you boys jabbering about?"

I poked a photograph with one grimy finger. "I think you'd better tell our pard everything."

So Mark told Tom about the Confederate raid on the San Francisco Mint and how we had stopped it. When he had finished, Tom just shook his head. "And you couldn't publish the story?"

Mark settled back against a wall. "Nope. The army thought the news would embarrass Lincoln almost as much as a successful robbery. The war was at a stalemate then. There were draft riots. And the fighting was getting so expensive the economy seemed likely to be ruined."

Tom looked at Mark as he were the biggest fool in creation. "In case you haven't heard, we've got freedom of the press in America."

Mark folded his hands over his lap. "They have to believe you first—even in America."

Tom rubbed his chin. "You mean, people would have thought you were just up to your old tricks?"

Mark had concocted a number of hoaxes when he'd written for a Nevada newspaper. The final one had gotten folks so mad that he'd had to leave the entire state.

"Something like that," Mark grunted.

Tom tapped a finger against his chest. "Well, we're partners now. I'll promise you one thing: Tom Sawyer never backed away from a fight with anyone—not even the U. S. Government."

Mark grunted. "It'll take more than a hose and pumper to handle the government."

Wanting to clean my fingers, I went back into the other room. The headlines on the newspaper on the wall proclaimed that Sheridan had just invaded Virginia's Shenandoah Valley and was burning everything in sight. When I picked up the first newspaper from the pile, I saw it was from the same day. So was the second and the third— though they were from different California cities. "Mark, Tom," I called, "why would anyone save all this?"

"Maybe he hated the Shenandoah." Tom began to riffle through the newspapers.

"Or maybe it made him hate," I suggested. "Major St. John said that the Shenandoah was his home. It's where his wife and children died." I got this real creepy feeling right at the back of my neck, like cold claws had just scraped across the skin.

Tangling with Major St. John had been plenty rough. He was the Confederate spy who'd hatched the plot to steal the gold in the San Francisco Mint. And it'd taken Mark and me and the entire United States Army to stop him. The major was so cold and calculating that he was beyond mean. He was a human shark.

"They never did find the major's body. Do you think he could still be around?"

"If he is," I said, "then Bobby's in with *real* bad company." Something clinked against my shoe. Bending over, I picked up a small blue bottle. There were two more bottles just like it, and there was blue glass against the wall, as if more bottles had been smashed.

I held the bottle so I could read the raised letters. "What's laudanum?"

Mark took the bottle from me. "It's a medicine that contains opium. That used to be Bobby's 'problem.'"

I sniffed at the bottle.

"Well, sometimes folks get powerfully attached to the stuff." He pocketed the bottle. "Poor Letty. I don't think Bobby's nearly as reformed as she thinks."

Tom clutched at Mark's arm. "Come on. I think we'd better get over to Tar Flat right away."

9

WE COULD SMELL TAR FLAT LONG before we saw it. The area stretched for about a mile, and you could see the smoke hovering over the gasworks.

Scattered among the ironworks and brass foundries were two-story rooming houses and little cottages that had either never been painted or the dirty air had eaten through the paint and gotten to the boards. Fences leaned out into the street or were missing planks. The whole neighborhood was like a watch winding down. I guess the people were too busy or too tired or too broke to care.

"Watch where you throw your matches," Tom cautioned Mark. "We're getting close."

"I could just light up the air and smoke that."

A woman in green shawl and ruffled bonnet was picking her way along the street. She was carrying a large carpetbag decorated with embroidered flowers.

"Letty?" Mark called.

"Mark, what are you doing down here?"

"I was going to ask the same thing."

Letty held up the carpetbag. "I got a note from Mr. Prescott asking me to bring the costumes to him at the gasworks. I'd do anything for Mr. Prescott. He was so kind to hire Bobby right away when he lost his job at Majestic."

Majestic Chemicals? That was some coincidence.

Before Mark or I could say anything, Tom stepped out and took Letty's arm. "We'll be passing by the gasworks ourselves. May we escort you?"

"You didn't come here for that," Letty said curiously.

Tom pulled at his mustache. "Let's just say that it's on our way."

The smell got worse the closer we got. Jets of flame would rise in the air, the excess gas being burned off. And all around the pipes and broken barrels and trash were patches of tar.

The gasworks covered a city block. Over the two-story buildings, I could just make out the masts of ships. The shot tower where they made gunshot was over on the corner; and there were sheds and shops for ironworkers and plumbers. They were all closed, though.

The oily dirt made squelching sounds under our feet, and twice it got so slippery I skittered and almost fell. A sudden turn brought us in sight of the gasworks. Mark had been right. It was the place where Prescott had taken all the pictures.

We passed a plumber's shop where a wagon with only three wheels was propped up on a box.

"There's Prescott's workshop." Letty pointed to a shack patched together with scraps of lumber and pieces of hammered tin. The raggedy tarpaper on the roof had rolled up like a cheap wig on a miser's bald head. The door was of heavy wood, but riddled with little holes. Termites or bullets—I couldn't say.

"It was so kind of you to come to renew an old acquaintance." A slight, blond man with a mustache stepped out from behind a building. He opened his ankle-length duster and pulled a navy colt from his waistband. Cocking the pistol, he aimed it in one smooth motion and waved the barrel for us to put up our hands.

Mark slowly raised his hand. "Major, we thought you were dead."

"Not so you'd notice," the major said, motioning us toward the shack. He nodded at Letty. "Sorry, my dear. I *must* insist that you all accept my hospitality."

The major smiled thinly. "I must apologize for the primitive conditions." The light came from a kerosene lamp, because there were boards nailed over the one broken window. There was a table and chairs and a cot against the wall. A pot of water was bubbling on a small potbellied stove.

"I have to thank you all for making things so easy for me. Letty, would you mind setting down your bag?" Letty had been silent all this time. I guess she was in shock.

"Where's Bobby?" Letty said suddenly. He's not coming, is he?"

The major studied Letty sadly. "Dear Miss Cleary, I'm afraid poor Bobby has had an accident. He perished in the fire at the chemical factory."

Mark shot a sympathetic glance at Letty. "What kind of accident did you arrange for Bobby? Did you do the same for Prescott, too?"

The major took a small suitcase from underneath the table. "Mr. Prescott sold me his business last year."

"I think we saw some of your handiwork in your studio. You really must like the gasworks."

The major set the suitcase down against the carpetbag and nudged the bags over toward the door with his foot. He was a cool one, all right.

The major swung his pistol toward Tom, who had started to lower his hand toward his boot.

He twisted the front door open and set the suitcases outside, then nodded at a pile of newspapers on the floor. "You people in San Francisco think you're safe; it's time you realized that the war will come looking for you no matter where you hide. Traitors like Clemens are the worst—Southerners who turn their backs on their kin and run away. I didn't ask those Yankees to murder my family. And now those butchers Sheridan and Sherman are plundering and killing on a scale that dwarfs anything I could do."

"Then let's stop the war now." Letty lunged toward the stove and reached to grab the pot handle, so she could fling boiling water at Major St. John.

The major's expression didn't even change when he fired. The roar of the gun sounded thunderous in the shack. Letty's body was flung sideways to the floor, and she didn't move.

Mark took a step toward the major, but he had already cocked the pistol again. "Stop right there."

"You're going to pay for this," Mark snarled.

"Undoubtedly. In the life after, if not this one. But I suspect that we will be sharing the same bench, Clemens." The major swept up his coat and bag and stepped outside.

Tom charged the door, but the major had already slammed it shut.

"Watch out," I yelled.

St. John's Colt exploded a second time, and splinters went flying from the door as a lead ball drilled a neat hole through the wood. A second later we heard the key turn in the lock.

Tom dug the pepperbox from his boot. "I wonder if I could kick that door down."

"Maybe there's some other way out," I said.

Mark was kneeling beside Letty.

Though her face was screwed up in terrible pain, Letty clawed at Mark's shirt. "Mark, he . . . Hop-Frog."

"Hop-Frog?" Mark asked.

Letty was a fighter. Her shoulders and chest rose as she tried to take one last breath.

"Letty?" Mark slid his hand beneath her neck. But her eyes widened, as if she were looking straight through him, and her hand dropped away. Mark closed her eyes. "Poor Letty. She deserved a whole lot better than this."

I could hear the water still bubbling on the stove. "We should never have let her come here," I said.

"We'll all be joining Letty pretty soon if we don't get out of here." Tom was standing to the right of the door as he aimed his pepperbox at the lock. There was a sharp crack as he fired, but when he shoved at the door, it wouldn't budge. "Either that's a mighty strong lock or there's some kind of bolt on the outside." Stowing his gun back inside his boot, Tom grabbed a chair and swung it over his head. "Maybe we'd better break through the window."

Tom gave a grunt as he brought the chair down hard, and the legs broke the last bits of glass and thudded against the boards. "A few more swings," he gasped, "and we'll be outside."

But then we heard the tinkling of glass, and the next moment we were sniffing the pungent smell of rotten eggs.

"Hurry," I yelled, running over to help Tom. But the boards still didn't break.

"Jehosophat." Tom raised the chair even higher, in the process almost lifting me from the floor. That's when the flames erupted and soared up beneath the window.

10

GLASS BEGAN TINKLING ALL AROUND us, and the smell of rotten eggs was overpowering. Flames crackled around the door and walls, small triangles at first, but they shot upward like bright weeds. The shack was already filling with smoke.

We began to swing the chair back and forth in rhythm, so that the legs hammered against the boards. By the sixth or seventh swing, a chair leg broke. And by the twelfth, the chair itself had caught fire.

We dropped it with a crash on the floor, and I got hold of a rag and whipped it against the burning chair leg. Now the boards of the cabin were outlined by fire—it seemed as if we were trapped inside a cell of glowing bars.

"Those boards were nailed to stay there till doomsday." Tom said.

"Maybe someone will see the fire," I said, "and get the fire companies."

Mark was doubtful. "Even if they did, how would they know we were in here?"

Once the fire reached the roof, the shack was going to collapse.

Tom looked up. "The roof. That's it."

He crouched, pointing his index finger toward a big brown stain in the center of the roof. "See that big patch of tin? Maybe we can knock it off and get out that way."

Tom and Mark had positioned the table underneath the tin patch. "Get Letty's shawl, will you?" Tom ordered.

Reluctantly, I eased the shawl out from underneath Letty. Her skin was still warm. Flames were starting to eat at the floor not more than a few inches from her. I wanted to drag her back, but those few seconds could make all the difference to us.

"Come on, Your Grace." Mark got the pot of

water and carefully poured it over the shawl.

Then Tom picked up the shawl and draped it over his head and shoulders. Water spattered down the wet fringes. "Stay close to the floor, Your Grace," he said. "More air there."

Tom swung a chair on top of the table and climbed up. "I think heaven is going to have to wait."

Mark eyed the flames. "Frankly, I expected to see a more southerly region in the hereafter."

Tom thrust the chair against the tin, and there was a hollow, bonging sound. "I think it's giving."

I beat at the flames on the floor, trying to keep them away from the table.

Tom was pounding at the tin, and the metal square boomed and echoed like we were in the middle of a thunderstorm. But by the tenth swing, we heard a crack.

"Was that a roof board?" Mark asked.

"No," Tom sounded grim, "it was a chair leg."

I was hopping around like a crazy frog, as I flailed at the fire on the floor.

Tom swung again and I heard another chair leg crack and fall off. He began to batter frantically at the tin. Suddenly he gave a sharp yelp.

I looked up to see a little rectangle of glorious blue sky. "You did it."

Tom lowered the chair and held out a hand to me. "Now, all you have to do is get outside and unlock the door for us."

I let myself be pulled up on the table with him. Under the double load, the table began to creak. "That hole looks awful small, Tom."

"Just think thin." Tom crouched on all fours.

The fire was beginning to spread across the roof as I climbed up on Tom's back.

"Can you get to the hole?" he grunted.

I stretched my arms, but there was still a whole yard between me and the hole. "It's just a little out of my reach."

Carefully, I repositioned myself with my legs over Tom's shoulders.

"Ready?" Tom gasped, and when I gave a little kick to Tom's side, he started to get to his feet. "Then hold on."

The fiery walls slid by as I rose into the air, swaying dangerously.

Tom wrapped his arms around my legs. "The table wasn't built for two acrobats."

The flames were only a yard away from the patch of tin, but I forced myself to reach up toward the hole.

"Stretch, Your Grace."

"I've got it," I shouted in triumph, as my fingers curled around the boards surrounding the opening.

Somehow Tom managed to grab the back of my thighs and boost me up.

Waves of heat rolled over my hands, so that my skin began to ache. Even so, I twisted and strained to slide through the gap. Flames licked at my face.

Shutting my eyes, I shoved my head on through. The hot tin burned my cheek. And then I was in the air and I gulped it in hungrily. I began to pull myself up through the hole. When I looked down again, Mark was setting his foot into Tom's hands. Mark gave a spring as Tom rose, and, with that extra boost from Tom, Mark caught hold of the edge of the hole.

"I got you." I reached through the hole and grabbed one of Mark's forearms.

"What a team," Mark panted, and began to pull himself up. Mark's red, sweating face popped into the air; but his shoulders wedged in the narrow opening.

"Too much high living, Mark." Though the tin was hot, I grabbed the edge and pulled until it screeched and bent.

"Right now I'd settle for a quart of grease so I could slick my way through." Jerking and wriggling, Mark began to slither free. When he was clear to his waist, he nodded to me. "Grab hold of my belt, Your Grace."

I let go of the tin, and it snapped against his hip. "Sorry," I said as I curled my fingers around his belt.

"Can you reach my legs, Tom?" Mark called below. "Or do you want me to lower myself a little?"

"Save yourself," Tom shouted. "I—" His voice was drowned out by a huge crash from within the shack.

"Tom!" I yelled. But there wasn't any answer.

"Wait. We'll take a look as soon as I get out," Mark said. He must have lost some of his personal hide on the tin, but he managed to get out of the hole.

As soon as Mark's feet had appeared, I looked over the edge into the shack. Tom was lying among the splintered remains of the table. I shouted to him again. He didn't move.

I looked around desperately from my high perch. In the distance, I could hear the bell ringing from the city hall tower, but there was no telling when the fire companies would get here. But men were running out of the gasworks now.

I tugged off my shirt and waved it like a flag. "Hey, up here."

One of the workers stopped and pointed to me. His voice came faintly over the distance.

Another man started to run back to the gasworks.

Mark cupped his hands around his mouth like a megaphone. "There's a man inside."

Mark pointed to the broken wagon in front of the plumber's shop and shouted, "Bring that wagon around and we can jump into that. Better get ready to leap, Your Grace."

"I've got to go back in to help Tom."

"You're a true noble, Your Grace. But once we're down on the ground, we can use that wagon as a battering ram. The walls ought to be almost burnt through."

"Maybe this heroism stuff is catching—like a cold." I just hoped that Mark's plan would work. I looked inside the shack, but Tom was only a dim shape in the smoke. Before Mark could stop me, I swung my legs back into the hole and let myself drop. I knew quite a bit about climbing and tumbling. A cat burglar named Mac had taught me. I tried to keep my legs together, and when I felt the first jarring contact with the floor, I relaxed and let myself roll.

Mark was shouting at me from above.

I scrambled over Tom. He was still breathing.

Outside the wagon rattled up to the shack. Mark's voice rose, and a moment later I heard a loud thump as he landed in the back of the wagon.

The table had broken in half, so that it arched on two sets of legs. Tom seemed awfully heavy as I tried to roll him onto his side. He blinked his eyes. "Just had the craziest nightmare."

"It's not over yet." Outside I could hear the creak and rattle of the wagon as it was swung around.

I pulled the table around, so it formed a kind of shelter for us.

The wagon boomed against the wall, and boards cracked and creaked in protest.

"Again," Mark shouted.

I could feel the rumbling in the ground as the wagon rolled back, and suddenly there was a huge explosion of splintering boards.

"Harder, boys," Mark was shouting. "Do it on a count. One."

A board crashed from the roof.

"Two."

Flames began to lick around the table.

"Three."

The wagon came crashing through. With a wall gone, the roof wasn't going to stay up much longer. I grabbed hold of Tom's arms—and almost got run over by the wagon.

"Whoa, boys. Whoa," Mark shouted. And I could see the men holding onto the hitching pole and the sides as they tried to drag it to a halt.

Tom sat up, dazed.

The blast of fresh air through the opening had made the flames roar even higher within the cabin. I grabbed Tom's shirt and tugged him toward the wagon.

Though still dizzy from his fall, Tom had enough sense to crawl with me to the wagon. We had just slid underneath the wagon bed when the roof crashed down. Still on all fours, we scrambled through the dirt underneath the wagon until we emerged at the front.

Mark was crouching there, holding onto the hitching pole. A broad, relieved grin spread over his face. "There has to be an easier way of writing a book."

11

BULLDOG BRILL WAS THE BEST DETEC-
tive on the whole police force. Folks
claimed you could show him the
feathers from a stolen chicken and he'd track the
thief down by sunset. But right at that moment,
he was staring at me angrily—as if I'd just con-
fessed to every murder in San Francisco for the
last ten years.

He puffed away at his cigar, like a locomotive
working up a full head of steam. "I'm disap-

pointed in you, Your Grace. I don't expect much common sense from these two fugitives from a dime novel. But I figured at least *you* would keep a level head. What's the idea of withholding evidence, Sawyer?"

Tom tried to give him one of those smiles that could charm a cat out of its skin. "It seemed like simple arson."

"And we know what a full case load you've got," Mark added.

"You pull any more of these stunts," Bulldog snapped, "and so help me, I'll stick you into a cell with the rottenest criminals I can find. And I'll throw away the key, too."

But if Bulldog thought mere words could shake up Tom, he had another thought coming. Tom's confidence was solid steel and sunk a mile into the ground. That grin of his just spread even farther across his face. "Want to bet I head up the gang by sunset?"

Bulldog gave a sniff and then another, and then his shoulders started to move and I realized he was chuckling. "I just bet you would."

Now that Bulldog was in a better mood, Mark dared to pluck at the sleeve of his tweed coat. Black braid was stitched around the hem and collar. "What happened? Did your old suit finally die of embarrassment?"

Bulldog Brill tugged at his red satin vest. "A fellow's got a right to dress up. And don't change the subject. We were talking about the major."

Mark wiped at a sooty spot on his cheek. "I just wish I knew what she meant by 'Hop-Frog.' "

Tom picked up a paperweight from Bulldog's desk. "Maybe it was something she was reading?"

Bulldog snatched the paperweight back from Tom and set it firmly back down on a stack of papers. He set his shoe on the seat of his chair and adjusted the brass buckle of one of his leather gaiters.

Mark looked at the ceiling, and I noticed the rectangular bulge in his pocket made by the book that Letty had loaned him. "Mark," I asked, "wouldn't Letty be thinking in terms of the writer that was most in her thoughts—what about the book the major gave her?" And I jabbed a finger at his pocket.

By the time we'd gathered around Mark, he'd taken out the book and was already running a finger down the table of contents. "Well," he said quietly. "Will you look at that?"

I peered over Mark's arm and saw his finger marking a story called "Hop-Frog." It was about a mean king who used to pick on one of his maids and a dwarf jester until they couldn't stand it anymore. So they hatched this plot and at a masquerade ball Hop-Frog and the maid set fire to the king and his men. "That Hop-Frog fellow sure got even, didn't he?"

Mark slammed the book shut. "There were newspapers at Prescott's with headlines about Sheridan's invasion of the Shenandoah Valley.

That used to be the major's home. I guess he wants to get even, all right."

Tom snapped his fingers. "Letty was loaning him costumes. We should look at the inventory. Maybe we can figure out what kind of disguises he'll be using."

"Just who's going to the premiere of the Pritchard's play?" I piped up.

Bulldog stroked his chin. "The richest and most important men in San Francisco."

Mark folded his hands together. "All gathered inside a place where they can burn together. It's very convenient for the major."

Tom let out a low whistle. "And Letty could have given him a costume that would have let him hide in the chorus."

With a sigh, Bulldog took his derby from a rack.

We all gave a little jump when someone tapped at the door. We could see the silhouette of a tall man who was so thin he might have been put together with a half-dozen sticks. "Officer Brill, it's me," he whispered urgently.

Bulldog reached a hand inside his coat for his gun. "Who's that?"

We could see the silhouette turn, as if the man were checking the corridor for eavesdroppers. "You know, Ted the florist. I hope you don't mind, sir. We were fresh out of daylilies. Would begonias be all right?"

I expected a lot of things from Bulldog—but romance? His cheeks were turning a ruddy, healthy red, as if he were blushing—and that was proof enough.

"Right, fine." Bulldog frantically tried to get rid of the florist, but it was already too late. The damage to his reputation had already been done.

"Fancy you taking an interest in nature." Mark reached out to chuck the policeman under the chin. "And if a man wants to get scented up like a bouquet himself—why, that's all up to him. But I'd never had taken you for a stage-door johnny."

Tom folded his arms across his chest. "I bet all those flowers cost a pretty penny. Does Cupid here go by the name of Shy Admirer?"

The florist clutched an order book against his chest, as if he would rather die than disclose the name. "I'm not at liberty to say."

Bulldog motioned us all outside, with big sweeps of his arms. I guess he didn't like having the tables turned so that he was the one being interrogated. "One investigation at a time," he growled.

It was dark by the time we all left the police station, and there was a real howler of a wind. Tom's face was grim. "This kind of wind could whip a fire through a whole city."

"Then we'd better catch the major before he can start one," Bulldog grunted.

Though the front doors to the opera house were shut, we could hear people talking in the side alley. We found Tartars and Poles taking a break from rehearsals. One fellow with a turban like a fat pumpkin was trying to keep his gigantic mustache from drooping down too low, while he puffed away hastily at a cigarette.

"Tartars didn't wear turbans, did they?" Mark asked Bulldog.

Bulldog marched straight up to a fellow with his hair in a top knot and a large scimitar thrust through his belt. "Where's Maguire?"

Top Knot jerked his head toward the opera house. "Having a drink. It seems that the Darling of Europe suddenly decided to do a benefit performance for some charity. We're going to have dress rehearsal without her."

When I heard a horse neigh from the back of an alley, I jumped. It wasn't the horse that pulled the red van, but this huge beast with legs as thick as street lamps. "What's he doing here?"

Top Knot's voice boomed in the alley. "Son, you're looking at the chief player in our little drama. That happens to be the Fiery Steed of Tartary himself. And he will take Miss Pritchard upon her Gallop to Death."

Mark tilted back his hat. "Y-a-a-s, well, I can see the death part, all right. That nag looks like it'll be lucky to survive the day."

"It's got a back as big as a bed," I protested. "It must have been used to pulling drays."

"So a little bitty thing like Miss Prichard shouldn't bother it at all. Well, will you look at that," Mark said, starting toward the mouth of the alley.

There, standing up in the back of a carriage

95

halted in the street, was a masked man, dressed in a fancy coat and satin pants that only came to his knees. His powdered wig had gotten knocked sideways while he tried to drape a blanket around the woman in the carriage. She was wearing a frilly, silver dress that must have been way too thin with that cold wind blowing. One hand tried to keep the tinsel crescent moon in her hair, and the other clutched a bow with a quiver of arrows.

My mouth dropped open. "Is that part of the show?"

Mark shook his head. "Wrong era. There must be a costume ball tonight."

The moment Mark said costume, something clicked in my head. "Maybe that's where the major was heading?"

Mark grunted. "And I'll just bet that the cream of society will be there tonight."

The wind blew off the man's wig. "It's a southern wind," Tom grimaced, "in more ways than one." A parasol sailed past, its frilly top gleaming a ghostly white in the light of the street lamps.

I shivered. "Then you can bet the major will take advantage of it."

Bulldog stared at the flame of his match. He shook it out before he even had a chance to light his cigar. "Then we'd better be on hand to stop him."

12

WHILE BULLDOG TRIED TO FIND OUT what he could about the costume ball, Mark and I went through the inventory books. Tom found disguises for us in Maguire's costume room. "Here," Mark said suddenly, and tapped a page.

I saw that someone had drawn a line through *Jester's motley, one.* "You mean like the jester in 'Hop-Frog'?"

"Open up," Tom shouted, kicking at the door.

I slammed my book shut and went to open the door. Tom was hidden behind a glittering pile of costumes. "What did you do? Steal the costume room?"

Tom staggered into the office. "You don't want to go in just any old thing, do you?"

I took Tom by the elbow and guided him over to the desk. "We want to catch the major, not win prizes for the best costumes."

"I only know one way to do things, and that's the right way." Tom spilled the costumes onto the desk top. "Do you think Bulldog will like being a pirate?" Tom held an eye patch up to one eye.

Mark sat back, as a plumed helmet bounded into his lap. "I think he'd prefer it to being a tin of beef."

Tom grabbed the helmet from Mark. "That's part of my costume. I'm going to be a knight." He patted a burlap shirt that had been painted silver.

Mark began to search through the pile, but Tom slapped his hand.

"I've got the perfect costume for you." Tom took out a small crown of gilt foil.

Mark felt the top of his head. "That looks a mite small."

Tom let the crown dangle from his fingers. "No, I'm afraid this is for someone else." Tom draped a knee-length tunic of velvet and gold thread over the back of a chair. "Here, Your Grace."

98

I suppose Tom thought I would enjoy dressing up like a prince, but I felt uncomfortable. "Don't you have anything besides this fancy getup?"

Mark saw how embarrassed I was. "Folks might not understand he was a real duke pretending to be a prince. They might think *both* were acts."

Tom dropped the crown on the desk. "Sorry, Your Grace. It was the only thing in your size."

I took the tunic and drew it over my head. It hadn't looked all that heavy, but it hung like a soggy blanket all around me. "What did you get for Mark?"

Tom made a circle with his thumb and index finger. "No one will recognize Mark in this outfit."

"Who is it? King Midas?"

Tom took out a long black gown and a short white tunic with wide sleeves. "This is called a cassock. And this," he flapped the white tunic, "goes over the cassock. It's called a surplice."

"I'm not going to be any altar boy."

"The costume ball's about to start," Bulldog called, as he came charging down the hallway. "It's supposed to raise money for the Sanitary Fund, to help wounded soldiers."

Tom held out a three-cornered hat and eye patch to Bulldog. "Where is it being held?"

"At the Chambers mansion." Bulldog put the eye patch in his pocket. "I want two eyes, so I can shoot straight. We'll have policemen around the mansion, but we're the only ones going. It'll mean my job if we're wrong."

"I'd feel a sight easier with more company," Mark complained.

Tom paused to look at Mark with a grin. "What could go wrong with Bulldog and me there?"

"Plenty," Mark said gloomily.

As we followed the carriages down the street, Mark kept his borrowed overcoat closed. "If this ever gets out, I'll lose whatever's left of my reputation."

Tom laughed through the visor on his helmet. "Who knows? You might have found your true calling."

"Don't like the hours. You have to get up too early on Sundays."

I suppose I should have tried to say something that would make Mark feel better, but I was too excited. I'd read about those society parties and I'd walked by big society mansions, but I'd never been inside one. When we got to the corner, I just had to stop and stare.

A long line of carriages waited patiently to let off their passengers in front of a mansion with fancy ornaments all around the facade. Wide marble steps led from the walkway to the front door, which had a roof supported by white columns.

It was like something from out of one of my own fantasies. "Is that the Chambers mansion?"

"It's really a house built around a ballroom," Mark said. Mrs. Chambers loves parties. She's a Southerner but tonight she's raising money for the North. To the major's way of thinking, that would make her a prime target."

Tom and Bulldog had gone on ahead, but I lagged behind to wet my hand and try to slick my hair down. I can't say that it did much good. "Mark, are these folks high society?"

"As close to American nobility as you can get. Mrs. Chambers is F. F. V.—First Families of Virginia."

If only I'd had some warning that I was finally going to be introduced into high society, I'd have tried to keep cleaner. Anyway, in all those books about lost heirs, it didn't matter what the child looked like—the true nobility of the soul shone through. I felt funny as we walked toward the gate—like I'd swallowed a can of itching powder.

A man in knee britches and a wig—just like servants in livery that I'd seen in pictures—was checking invitations. We had to wait behind a man in hose and brocade, and also a woman with blonde hair that floated over her mermaid costume of blue-green tulle with bits of lace sewed on to imitate coral.

Bulldog fished out his badge and stepped ahead of another couple. "My men and I have reason to suspect a criminal may be at this party."

"If he's got an invitation, he can get in. If he

doesn't have an invitation, then he can't."

"But I'm the police." Bulldog waved his badge like a magic wand.

"So's the chief. And he's already inside."

Mark put his hand on Bulldog's shoulder.

"This calls for a different approach. You're not raiding some gambling den now."

The servant peered around Bulldog. "Mark, is that you?"

"Hallo, Jimmy. I never expected to see you in that getup. Have you seen anyone dressed as a court jester? Blonde fellow?"

Jimmy thought for a moment. "No. There are a lot of jesters here—and a lot of wigs." He jerked a thumb at Mark's overcoat. "If you want to get in, let's see your costume first."

"Isn't my word good enough?"

"You've seen me in this monkey suit. I want to see you in yours."

"Come on, Mark," Bulldog growled. "You've got to take the coat off inside."

Mark turned beet red but undid the buttons.

Jimmy laughed out loud.

Mark quickly wrapped his overcoat around himself again. "I don't think these colors flatter me."

Jimmy stepped aside with a mock bow. "Tell the guys at the door I say you're okay. But watch out for a fellow that looks like this." Jimmy squinted and pressed his lips together as if someone had just pinched his nose. "He's the head butler."

Mark waved Bulldog and Tom past us. "I won't forget this."

"Neither will I, Mark," Jimmy chuckled. "Not to my dying day."

At the top of the steps, Jimmy's message got us through the door, though the maid who took Mark's coat looked at us doubtfully.

"Well, welcome to the good life, Your Grace," said Mark.

The floor of the lobby was marble so polished that I could see myself. A flight of stars with gilt banisters swept upstairs, and on either side were mirrors in heavy gold frames. The cornices and moldings had been shaped to look like angels and devils. And overhead was a high-domed ceiling with paintings of folks running around in colored sheets and rolling their eyes like cows needing a milking. "Who're those folks and what's their trouble?" I asked.

Mark craned his neck and then rubbed his throat in a leisurely fashion. "History, mainly. They're famous folks from Greek and Roman times." He looked down at me. "And you call yourself a well-read person."

"My mother didn't have those kind of books." I looked around at the walls of the lobby, and there were more cow-eyed folks with funny pantaloons on their legs and wide cloth circles around their necks. And they were looking sterner than a sidewalk preacher on Good Friday. "And who're those folks with the funny collars?"

"The collars are called ruffs." Mark held out his palm toward one painting of a fellow with a sharp-pointed beard. "And that, Your Grace, is an artist's idea of the great Shakespeare himself." He swept his arm around in a circle. "And the rest of these are the playmates of his imagination."

"They don't look like very sociable types," I said, as I spun around on my heel. I stopped when I saw the smirk on the maid's face. I guess she'd overheard us.

Mark gave a chuckle. "Considering that a lot of them wind up dead by the end of the evening, I guess that would be an accurate judgment."

From the ballroom to our right, I could hear the orchestra playing a lively tune. "That's pleasant enough foot-tapping music," I observed.

"It's a *galop*," someone snickered. It was the maid who'd smirked at us when we came in.

In my daydreams, I'd always fit in naturally with the high-toned crowd. But it wasn't working out like that. So much for the true nobility of my soul. It sure wasn't shining through.

Mark drew me toward the threshold of the ballroom. The high ceiling and windows made the room seem big as a barn. The dancers moved under a glittering chandelier. Baskets of flowers scented the air, while cages of birds sang counterpoint to the orchestra.

Mrs. Chambers was dressed as the Queen of

Hearts, in red velvet trimmed with black satin. Gold, silver, and diamonds were showered over the costume.

A little man trailed her proudly—like a small boy with the best-saddled pony. Mark whispered, "And *that* is Mr. Chambers?

"*There's a jester.*" Bulldog began to ease his way through the crowd toward a man in a red-and-blue fool's cap. "Sir." He grabbed the jester's shoulder and pullled him around.

But it was some fellow with a thin mustache waxed so stiff that it looked like a knitting needle. He wiped at the champagne that had spilled when Bulldog yanked him. "You might have at least let me have a sip first."

A disappointed Bulldog shoved his way back through the throng to us. "I think we'd better split up. Your Grace, you come with me. And you"— he flicked a nail against Tom's helmet with a tinny clink—"if you find the major, you leave him to me. Just because you're dressed like a knight in shining armor doesn't mean you are one."

13

I N THE NEXT HALF-HOUR, BULLDOG AND I
found two more jesters in the crowd, but they
weren't the major.

There were at least a half-dozen Henry the VIII's
and other kings like Richard the Lionhearted, and
some ladies Bulldog said were supposed to be
dressed up like daughters of the regiment after
some opera.

"Try not to point," Bulldog whispered. "That's
General McDowell, head of the Department of the

Pacific. He's supposed to be Charles the Second of England. The woman he's dancing with is supposed to be Anne Boleyn, one of Henry the Eighth's wives." A ruff of starched cloth, big as a saloon tray, surrounded her neck, and bell-shaped sleeves covered her hands. Even her feet were hidden by her long gown.

We met Mark and Tom back at the refreshment table, where they were both getting champagne.

Mark shook his head when Bulldog asked if he'd had any luck.

"Letty brought the major more than one costume," Bulldog continued. "He could be in some other outfit."

Mark frowned at the whirling dancers. "In fact, he could be almost anyone at this confounded ball—assuming that he's even here."

"Watch out; we have trouble coming up on the starboard side." Tom nodded toward the butler with the pinched face who was striding toward us.

"Where's the chief?" Bulldog growled.

"Too late for that," Tom said softly. And then in a loud voice, he declared to Mark, "I've got every right to be here."

If I didn't do something quick, all four of us would be dusting off the sidewalks with our backsides, so I picked up on Tom's cue. "Now see here, my good man," I said in my best accent, "may we see your invitation?"

"Well, my pard's got it." Tom pretended to scan the crowd. "But I don't see him right now."

"Then," the butler took Tom's arm, "I suggest you wait outside." The butler still seemed to be eyeing us as well, so I pointed my finger accusingly at Bulldog. "And I don't think this one has an invitation, either."

"Really?" The butler hesitated and then added, "Sir?" We were safe for the moment.

Mark was quick to add, "Really, we have not come here to mix with riffraff from the streets."

I raised my hand haughtily. "Chambers, I say, Chambers—"

The butler nodded his head. "There's no need, sir. I'll take care of it."

"Well, see that you do." I adjusted my tunic. Maybe I wasn't so out of place here, after all. I should have started using my accent sooner.

The orchestra ended its piece and Mrs. Chambers stepped up on the podium, but everyone went on talking until a Henry the VIII began clanking a spoon against a champagne glass. "Thank you. Thank you." She beamed at the Henry. "I and"— she nodded to Mr. Chambers—"wish to thank you for attending our charity *bal masqué* tonight for our brave boys in blue." She paused to bow at the scattering of applause; she looked ready to bow again, but the applause stopped too soon.

"As you know, we were originally planning to auction off a barrel of Hawaiian molasses. Several weeks ago one fetched twelve hundred dollars." The applause was a little more heartfelt when money was mentioned, but Mrs. Chambers accepted it for herself and smiled prettily. "I just wanted to tell you that we've found something much sweeter than molasses. You know that all San Francisco has been abuzz over the arrival of one special person, who has finally returned to us after triumphs all over Europe and the States. And Mrs. Pritchard has consented to auction off kisses."

"The very idea," a woman in a two-foot-high white wig was saying on my left. "How dare they bring that scarlet woman here?"

The Pritchard had waltzed out of a back room. On top of her head was a white turban, and she wore a short blue jacket with red braid. Her baggy red trousers were tucked into spats. Behind her, like a sullen caboose, came Sir Eustace, dressed like a clown.

As soon as the applause died down, Mrs. Chambers started to open her mouth, but the Pritchard beat her to it. "Thank you, San Francisco." Waving a gavel over her head, the Pritchard stepped up on the podium and all but shoved Mrs. Chambers off of it. "I'm so glad to be back in my favorite city in the world."

"Humbug," Mark muttered. "I've heard her give that same speech in Nevada, but that time her favorite place was Virginia City."

The Pritchard clasped the gavel in both hands. "But before we begin the auction, I want to perform a selection of Shakespeare's soliloquies."

An alarmed Mrs. Chambers tried to climb back up on the podium; but the Pritchard neatly stepped in front of her, blocking her way. "There's always time for some of the Bard." She handed the gavel to Sir Eustace. "My first piece will be the dreadful Lady Macbeth." Her head dipped abruptly, and she raised her right arm so that her forearm was resting against her forehead—like a bird trying to hide its head under its wing.

"Doesn't she mean 'dreaded'?" I whispered.

"No, I've seen her on stage. *Dreadful* is right."

"That's unkind, Clemens. Supposing people told you what they thought of your writing?" There was only one person I'd heard call Mark by his given name of Sam Clemens.

From the corner of my eye, I saw the snubnose of a single-shot derringer poking out of the huge right sleeve of Anne Boleyn. With his mustache shaved off and wearing makeup, Major St. John made a pretty woman.

"You," I gasped.

"You know," the major cocked his derringer, "the two of you are becoming quite tiresome."

Stalling for time, I said, "I have to hand it to you, Major. You've got your nerve dancing like that with General McDowell himself."

"He wasn't bad," St. John observed, "Once I remembered to let him lead." He gestured with his free hand toward a vacant chair. "Please put your drink down. Slowly . . . if you don't mind."

"It's no use, you know. We know about your plot. We've got this whole area cordoned off, and the fire companies have all been alerted."

110

St. John slid his sleeve over his right hand. "It still should make interesting headlines back in the States." His voice became harsher. "Shall we go, gentlemen?"

"We're not worth much as hostages." Mark began to move forward. "After all, the Duke hasn't come into his inheritance, and I'm only a second-rate reporter, after all."

"You underestimate yourself, Clemens." St. John motioned me to join Mark. "I've heard you owe so much money that half the city's economy would collapse if I shot you."

"Let's not stretch the truth," Mark said, as we began to make our way through the crowd. It's been considerably bent by other folks."

"This is no lie, Clemens." The major slid his arm through mine. "The boy will die if you don't do exactly what I say."

14

MAJOR ST. JOHN GUIDED US TOward the rear of the ballroom, where a flight of servants' stairs angled upward. "The war's lost, Major," said Mark. Our footsteps echoed in the stairwell. "Why don't you face facts?"

The major let go of my shoulder. He'd taken off the headdress that had hidden his hair and was using it to wipe the makeup from his face. "The war may be lost, but there is still one thing left."

"Peace?"

St. John ripped off the wide ruff that had covered his chest as well. "No, Clemens—revenge."

"But how could you use a sweet, trusting soul like Letty?" I asked.

At the first landing, the major waved Mark over to the next flight of stairs. The next moment he gripped my shoulder and pressed the muzzle against my neck. "What's the death of one silly woman? Or a few dozen, even a hundred? In the war, thousands of men die in one afternoon."

St. John ripped his skirt from bodice to hem. Underneath he was wearing red-and-blue checkered pantaloons rolled up to his knees. "I'm a surgeon compared to a butcher like Grant."

"But what if the fire spreads?" Mark demanded. "There are women and children in this city."

"What about the women and children of Atlanta? And the Shenandoah?" Pulling the skirt from his waist, he gently lowered it to the landing.

A dozen small bottles had been sewn into a row of pockets along the inner lining of the skirt. Mark gave a low whistle. "Say, wasn't it dangerous to sashay around on the dance floor wearing those things?"

"I accepted only slow dances." The major removed the bodice of the dress to reveal a checkered tunic that matched his pantaloons. "I could have run away like you, Clemens. But I choose to fight for what I believe in." The major carefully gathered up the corners of his skirt to make it into a heavy sack.

Mark shook his head. "When is this madness going to stop?"

"When one side cries enough. And if the North wins, I intend to see that at least one city weeps for that victory."

At the next landing, we walked quickly and quietly over the plush carpets toward a room with double doors. "You should be quite comfortable . . . up till the time of your deaths."

We found ourselves in a room where a huge bed sat majestically under a pink silk canopy supported on its four posts. Everything in the room was pink—the walls, the rugs, the curtains, the chairs, and the dressing table.

Mark blinked. "I've never seen anything so relentlessly pink before."

"I'm sorry that I couldn't arrange for a more tasteful death chamber." The major shoved me toward the bed. "Twist the sheets into ropes. And if you're not quick about it, I'll shoot Clemens here and see that you die even more unpleasantly."

"We're going to die one way or another," Mark countered.

"I'm not as cruel as you seem to think, Clemens. I'm willing to give you a sporting chance." He nodded toward the dressing table. A small blue bottle tilted off the table's edge. It would have fallen except for the white string tied to the gilt frame of the mirror above the dressing table. Beside the string sat a candle with wax lumped around its base. It had only a fraction of an inch left to go before it would begin burning the string. When the string broke, the bottle would drop onto a half-dozen more bottles massed at the foot of the dressing table.

"It's crude," the major said apologetically, "but simple to carry and set up, as you can see. Now, the longer you dally, the less time you will have to try to get free."

Together Mark and I stripped the bed down to the sheets, which had also been dyed pink.

The major was standing between us and the nearest window. There was no way I could think of to signal to Tom and Bulldog.

I began to run over things that Mac had told me about escaping. He had not only been good at ac-robatic falls, but he'd known a few magic tricks as well—sleight of hand had been a hobby with him. He'd once escaped from the police, though he'd had a set of manacles around his ankles and a pair of handcuffs around his wrists. And then I knew what to do. When we were finished with the sheets, the major ordered me to stand at the foot of the bed. I took a deep breath.

He had Mark tie me to one of the posts. "Tighter," the major barked, and Mark had to obey. The major checked it and then quickly tied Mark to the other bedpost.

He stepped back, surveying his handiwork with approval. "I'm afraid, gentlemen, that my adieu must be a quick one." He took out a flat cap with three peaks and, lowering the hammer on his derringer, tucked the gun into his waistband.

"How many other contraptions like this have you rigged up?" Mark called after him.

"I wouldn't worry about the two others, Clemens. I very much doubt you will be able to escape this one." He gave us a jaunty salute as he picked up the sack of little bottles and left the room, shutting the door carefully behind him.

All this time I had been taking quick, little breaths to keep my chest expanded. Now I let all the air out of my lungs in one explosive sigh—and the sheet-rope sagged a little around me.

"So that's what you were up to." Mark nodded his approval. He glanced at the dressing table. "Better hurry, Your Grace."

I began to wriggle my shoulders and back and arms—like a snake that had its tail set on fire. *Make your bones like rubber,* I told myself. *Like rubber!*

"Hurry," Mark urged. "The string is starting to turn brown."

"Did you have to tie the knots so tight?" My hands tugged at the top knot and finally it began to come loose. The dressing table was ten feet away. But I just managed to hook my heel on the bedspread where we had dropped it and drew it toward me.

"The string's starting to fray," Mark's voice broke in.

As I felt the final knot give, I just slid to the floor

through the sagging loops of the sheet. Grabbing the bedspread, I gathered it into a huge ball in my arms.

"Get out, Your Grace!" Mark yelled.

With both hands, I threw the bedspread toward the dressing table. It slid backward over the bottles beneath. I heard a clink, but there was no rotten egg smell; I had knocked the bottles over without breaking them. And even as I watched, the blue bottle dropped off the edge of the dressing table. The string fluttered behind as it plopped harmlessly onto the bedspread.

HURRY UP AND UNTIE ME, YOUR GRACE. We've got two more contraptions to disarm."

We could hear the distant sound of merry shouts from below. Barrie Pritchard was probably conducting the auction for her kisses. The folks downstairs were having a high old time. They'd be singing a different tune if Mark and I didn't find the major's calling cards.

I yanked open the first door on the right side of

the hall. Mark was taking the left side. Everything looked like it should, so I went on to the next room.

I had checked a half-dozen more before I found the major's next little trick, a bottle set on the edge of a chair in a walk-in linen closet. Sheets had been piled up so that the fire would have plenty of fuel. I carefully took the bottle and set it on the chair. Blowing out the candle, I darted down into the hallway again. "Found one," I called. But there were an awful lot of rooms in the Chambers mansion. It didn't seem like we'd ever find the last contraption, even if the major was telling the truth about there only being two more. I'd gone through a dozen rooms when Mark sang out, "I got it." It was on a shelf in a closet; dresses were heaped all around.

"The major uses mighty expensive kindling for his fires." In Mark's hand was a bottle with a brown string tied to it.

I let myself sag against a hallway wall.

"Let's just check a few more rooms." Mark started down the hallway.

I went into what seemed to be a study. I was so intent on bottles that I almost didn't notice the large gap on one wooden shelf, as if half the books had disappeared.

I circled around the big mahogany desk and saw the bottle tied to the knob of a drawer. It would be seconds before it fell on the books and papers scattered on the floor.

"Mark, in here," I shouted, but it was the pinch-faced butler who stormed through the doorway, instead.

The butler had the grip of a boa constrictor. "Let go of me. I'm trying to save you from a disastrous fire," I shouted.

"I've heard a lot of alibis, but this takes the prize."

"I'll collect it later." Putting all my weight on my right leg, I swung my left leg around so that it caught the butler behind his knee.

He toppled backward and there was a solid *thunk* as his skull hit the hard wood of the desk. I dove for the bottle and just managed to wrap my hands around it, as a paperweight fell off the desk onto the pile of books.

I just lay there on the floor trying to convince my lungs to start breathing again.

"Your Grace?"

"Over here. I had a visitor."

"So I see." Mark felt the butler's pulse. "Well, he's alive, but I think he's going to have a headache when he wakes up."

Mark peered out the window. "Hey, there's Tom and Bulldog." He tugged at the window and it rattled up. Mark shouted as he poked his head outside, "You—Tom, Bulldog. The major may be down below."

I saw Tom race across the street to the mansion. Bulldog motioned to the other policemen and plunged after him. Nothing—neither Jimmy nor the head butler—would stop them now.

"What makes you think the major will still be around, Mark?"

"He'll want to start fires by the doors to the ballroom to cut off escape. And he would certainly wait for the fires to get going up here before he started setting them down below."

Mark hooked an arm through mine and steered me toward the front stairs. "Come on. Maybe we can flush St. John so he'll run straight into Tom and Bulldog. They ought to suspect anyone in a jester's outfit—especially if he's running."

We could hear folks shouting and laughing at the auction. "One hundred dollars," boomed one man enthusiastically.

"A hundred and fifty."

"Gentlemen, gentlemen," the Pritchard was saying. "This is the last kiss I will bestow tonight. Surely it's worth more."

"Mark, by the door." I pointed to the red-and-blue checkered sleeve.

"Two twenty-five," a man was yelling from the ballroom.

Mark stopped and turned his back to the foot of the stairs. "Well, here goes nothing, Your Grace." Flinging a leg over the banister, he began to slide down.

The marble top of the banister felt mighty cold when I sat down on it. My reflection in the lobby mirrors seemed to be flashing through the air. Down below, I heard a thump and a groan, but I didn't dare look.

The next moment Mark grabbed me and twisted me off the banister before I hit the cupid at the bottom.

I eyed the sharp arrow in the cupid's bow. "How did you miss hitting that thing?"

Mark rubbed his backside. "I didn't. But luckily something broke my fall."

The footman lay sprawled on the floor. "Is that the 'something'?"

"Pretty hard on Mr. Chambers's help, aren't we?"

"They should be getting hazard pay," I agreed as I sprinted after him into the ballroom.

16

"FIVE HUNDRED. WHO'LL MAKE IT FIVE hundred for my last kiss of the evening?" There seemed to be no takers at that steep price, and the Pritchard was getting annoyed.

"Got you," Mark cried in triumph, when he grabbed the jester.

It was the fellow with the waxed mustache again. Champagne from his glass had spilled all over him. He raised a plate with some kind of flaky pastry on it, and with a flip of his wrist, dumped it on top of Mark's head. "There. How do you like that?"

Mark sniffed the air. "I've always been partial to salmon."

"A salmon bouché, to be exact," the man said, and sipped the last of the champagne in his glass.

"Indeed." Mark dipped his head and brushed off as much of the fish and pastry flakes as he could, but a lot was still tangled in his dense, red curls. "I must remember to try another of those. Maybe this time I'll get to eat it."

I caught a glimpse of red and blue over by the French doors, but when I turned my head, all I could see were women in two-foot-high white wigs and tent dresses.

"This is not for my vanity, gentlemen," the Pritchard was scolding the crowd. "It's for charity."

At that moment we saw a red-and-blue peaked cap appear from behind one of the wigged women.

"Stop," Mark shouted.

The Pritchard gave a triumphant cry. "It's sold for five hundred. Going . . ." The Pritchard's voice rose higher. "Going . . ."

Mark half ran, half slid across the well-waxed dance floor, but he managed to reach the French doors with me right behind.

"Gone!" the Pritchard shouted exultantly, "to the gentleman with the curly red hair."

Heads swiveled around and I couldn't help

staring, too. What fool would bid five hundred dollars for a kiss? Everyone was looking at Mark.

"They think that you've just bought that kiss."

"Aren't they in for a surprise when it comes time to get paid." Mark plunged straight toward the startled ladies; like top-heavy wagons, it was only with difficulty that they moved to either side to reveal Major St. John.

"We've spoiled your little game, Major. The police will be here any moment."

The major raised his hand to reveal a blue bottle in his fist. He still had his deadly sack with him. "The game isn't over until I'm dead."

"Oh, now, don't be shy," the Pritchard coaxed. "Come up and collect your prize."

With a sudden lunge, Mark caught the major's wrist before St. John could throw the bottle down.

"We-ell," the Pritchard announced with mock indignation. "I guess he'd rather waltz with that jester than collect a kiss from me. How about a little music for them?" A couple of violins started some sappy song, and the rest of the orchestra joined in.

"This man's a Confederate agent," Mark shouted desperately. But between the music and the laughter that filled the ballroom, I barely heard it and I was only a few feet away.

As they shuffled around on that slick floor, each of them trying to brace his feet, it looked in fact as if they were doing a very clumsy dance.

I rushed to the French doors that opened onto the verandah and twisted the handles, so that the doors suddenly swung open. "Mark, over this way."

I saw Mark try to shove the major outside, but the major was just as determined to keep them inside. Mark was going to need help, so I stepped back through the doorway, grabbed hold of his cassock, and yanked. Mark's skirttails came through the door first, followed by Mark and the major.

The three of us went spinning across the narrow verandah. My legs came up against something low and hard, and I went tumbling backward through the air. My head thumped against the lawn.

"Your Grace," Mark shouted. There was a meaty *thwack* of a fist hitting something, and then Mark was falling through the air after me.

The major stood against the balustrade over which Mark and I had just fallen. "This is the last time I underestimate you, Clemens." He lifted the bottle menacingly.

Mark looked around desperately for Bulldog and Tom, but there was no one. "Let the boy go. What can he do?"

"He's done enough already."

"I intend to do more." My groping hand felt the hard, boxlike lines of some object. It was Letty's copy of Poe. It must have dropped out of Mark's pocket when he fell. I curled my fingers around it—someone had to stop Major St. John.

"The first bottle will be for you, boy. The next for Clemens."

Bulldog appeared on the verandah with his Smith and Wesson .22 breechloader already cocked. "Hands up, Major. You can't get away now."

Tom was right behind him, his pepperbox aimed at the major. "A smart man knows when to quit."

"Take one step closer," the Major warned, "and the boy dies."

"He'll do it, Bulldog," Mark cried.

Bulldog stopped where he was, but he didn't lower his gun. "What do you want?"

The major kept his eyes on me. "A carriage and no one following me. I'll let the boy go when I know I'm safe."

"What makes you think I'd trust you?" Bulldog demanded, but there was a note of resignation in his voice.

"You'd have my word as a gentleman." The major was looking straight at Bulldog and Tom.

I whipped my arm through the air with all my strength and flung the book toward the major's head. St. John easily stepped aside, but he forgot about his sack of bottles. The book just clipped the bottom of the bag.

There was a soft clunk, and a small tuft of flame sprouted from the sack. The verandah reeked of rotten eggs. A fraction of a second later, I heard a series of crystalline notes, as if more bottles were breaking from the heat. And then the entire sack disappeared in a large ball of flame, which now engulfed St. John's left arm and shoulder.

The bottle went flying from his hand as he desperately beat at the flames, and then he snatched his right hand away as his right sleeve also caught fire. The bottle shattered on the lawn, bursting into flame a moment later.

"Fall to the ground and roll," Mark shouted.

But the major was past understanding.

The music faltered and stopped in the ballroom, as folks tried to crowd out on the verandah. Major St. John pirouetted slowly, slowly on the balls of his feet, fluttering his arms as he circled in a slow, deadly waltz. When he fell over and hit the lawn, he lay on his back, kicking and waving his arms like some tortured beetle.

"Good Lord," Tom murmured as he jumped down beside us.

"I wouldn't have wished this death on anyone, even the major."

Mark tried to beat at the flames with his surplice, but the flimsy cotton caught fire in his hands. He let it go and it seemed to float in the air, a bright moth of flame that vanished before it could touch the ground.

I started to yank my tunic off as I ran toward the major, but suddenly he let out a shrill, high scream that froze me in midstep.

Bulldog pointed his gun.

I turned away. It was only seconds, but the screaming seemed to go on and on and on before I heard Bulldog cock the hammer.

And then Bulldog fired and the screaming stopped.

17

M ARK LOOKED AT ME AND TOM. "I don't know. What do you think, pards?" It's a heady thing to have the head of the entire Department of the Pacific beg for a favor.

"If this story gets out," General McDowell said, "mobs will be lynching anyone with a drawl." A squad of police had already heaved the major's canvas-shrouded body into the back of a wagon. More policemen were spreading dirt over the smoldering lawn.

Tom took off his helmet and cradled it in the crook of his arm. He had once bragged that he wouldn't back down before anyone—not even the U. S. government—and he was as good as his word now.

Tom pointed to his left temple. "See the white hairs, Bulldog? See them? Every one is due to the major. Someone owes me for them."

"A little cheap shoe polish will work wonders," Bulldog growled.

"But what about Letty?" I broke in. Tom was going to find me just as stubborn as he was. "You know, in the end, Letty was a lot more noble and heroic than a lot of kings and queens. It seems wrong to make money from her death—especially when we helped cause it."

"Even if we hadn't happened along, the major would never have let her go." Tom played with the plume on his helmet. "I'm just as sorry about Letty as you are. But, hang it all, Your Grace, we just tracked down a dangerous Confederate spy. People owe us at least a proper thank-you."

Mark slapped his notebook against his palm while he considered. "Maybe it's time to admit that writing isn't for me—not if I have to write about folks like Letty getting killed."

"I must have gotten a powerful lot of dirt in my

ears," Tom said. "You're not quitting the whole writing business now?"

Mark tossed his notebook into an ornamental shrub. "I can always try my hand at mining again."

"Aren't you boys tired of risking your necks to save the city and getting nothing for it?"

"Is that why you stopped the major?" I gave Tom a poke. "For the money and the glory? Or did you do it because it was worth doing?"

"Come on, Tom," Mark coaxed. " 'Fess up. Writing about this arson case would be making Letty into a victim all over again."

"Well, I guess I would feel like more of a skunk than a hero."

I nodded to Bulldog. "You can tell the general there that the vote's unanimous."

Bulldog patted my shoulder. "I knew I could depend on you to do the noble thing." He went off with the general to speak to him alone.

I rubbed a dirt streak from the front of my tunic. I'd had my little taste of the high life, and I can't say I cared for it much—not if I had to deal with snooty maids and head butlers and stuck-up, useless fools like Sir Eustace. The heavy tunic was beginning to feel too hot, so I slipped one arm out of its sleeve.

Mark had begun to search under the shrub for his notebook. It had been a short retirement, after all. He brushed the dirt from the notebook cover as he came back toward us.

I slipped my other arm free from the tunic. It was strange. When I took off that tunic, I suddenly felt as if I'd just shed fifty pounds.

The three of us fell silent. Above the flickering street lamps, the clouds gleamed almost silver against a small patch of blue-black sky.

"I can't make out more than two stars," Mark sighed, and turned to me. "There's nothing like a riverbank at night, with the sound of water in your ears"—Mark swept his hand over his head— "and overhead a night sky full of stars."

Well, we had better than a river. We had a whole ocean just a few miles away. And I felt a need to get away now to anyplace but this city. "Maybe I could sign as a cabin boy on some ship. Put all the duke-ing aside."

Mark nodded. "It's a hard life, but no harder than the one you've led so far. Who knows? Maybe I'll even be joining you."

"Well, don't look at me," Tom said. "I've had my fill of being a sailor."

"And in the meantime," Mark grinned, "I'll see to it that Bulldog treats us to a five-course meal somewhere. Or else everyone will know the identity of the Shy Admirer."

"That's blackmail."

Mark tweaked my ear. "We can't always be virtuous."

Tom said, "I vote we have dinner at Martin's Restaurant, with quails and steaks falling off our platters."

Mark found the slit in the side of his cassock and slipped his notebook into his pocket. "Why not? Don't heroes deserve the best?" He winked at me. "Even if folks don't know about it."